Guardians of the Dark

Smoke on the Water

BIANCA D'ARC

This book is a work of fiction. The names, characters, places, and incidents are products of the writer's imagination or have been used fictitiously and are not to be construed as real. Any resemblance to persons, living or dead, actual events, locale or organizations is entirely coincidental.

No part of this book may be used or reproduced in any manner whatsoever without written permission, except in the case of brief quotations embodied in critical articles and reviews.

1st Edition
Copyright © 2011 Bianca D'Arc
Published by Kensington Publishing, Inc.

2nd Edition
Copyright © 2019 Bianca D'Arc
Published by Hawk Publishing, LLC

Copyright © 2019 Bianca D'Arc

All rights reserved.

ISBN-13: 978-1-950196-06-7

An eerie mountain lake will bring them together in scintillating passion...or tear them apart. Literally.

The most dangerous trail of his career...

In the misty fog of a lakefront dotted with vacation cabins, zombies are roaming wild - and CIA operative turned zombie hunter, John Petit, must stop the carnage. He's paired with a fresh-faced recruit brought to the team more for her immunity to the zombie contagion than any particular skill.

She never asked for any of this...

Donna was attacked and lived to tell the tale. One of the rare few who are naturally immune, she's part of the top secret team trying to stop the spread of this alarming technology. She doesn't want to let her partner down - especially in light of the fact that the more they're together, the more she's attracted to him.

A passion they cannot deny...

Facing danger together only adds fuel to the fire of need between them. Their chemistry is explosive, but will it fizzle in the harsh light of day? Or, can it last past the heat of the moment, once they've neutralized the deadly threat that endangers all humanity?

PRAISE FOR BIANCA D'ARC

"Definitely love my experience with this lady's books will definitely be reading more..." - *Late Night Sexy Book Reviews* on *Smoke on the Water* in **The Beast Within** anthology

"Zombies and spies, oh my!" - *GoodReads* reviewer on **The Beast Within**

"I love that John can be alpha, but still understand Donna and try to accommodate her. He even admits being wrong! *swoon*" - *GoodReads* reviewer on **The Beast Within**

Read the complete *Guardians of the Dark* series:
1. Simon Says
2. Once Bitten
3. Smoke on the Water
4. Night Shade
5. Shadow Play

AUTHOR'S NOTE & DEDICATION

Note: This is the second edition of this story, which first appeared as part of *The Beast Within* anthology alongside stories by Erin McCarthy and Jennifer Lyons. The title of this story has not changed, but it was previously published under the anthology title. Apologies for any confusion this re-release might cause.

I'd like to thank my dear friend, Peggy McChesney who helped me whip these books into shape. The editing they received in their first publication was…um…not all it could have been. There were reasons for that. I had just lost my mother and my brain was not at its best. The publishing house was going through a major upheaval as one of the grand dammes of the New York publishing world suddenly died and her young assistant was left to pick up the pieces.

Then a new regime came in and cleaned house, taking that young assistant—who was my editor—with it, and as a result, me and my poor little books never quite got the attention I felt they deserved. In fact, it's amazing they were even published at all with everything that was going on both at the publisher and in my personal life at that time.

Now that I have control of these books back, I'm fixing the errors that slipped through and I'm sorry to say there were some doozies! Mostly, they were continuity errors and I'm doing my best to eliminate them with Peggy's help. She did her best. If any mistakes remain, it's totally my fault because I have to admit, I am definitely getting confused. My process is to write as clean as possible in the first draft so as to avoid just this kind of confusing situation later.

That said, I believe we've done a good job on these second editions and hope you will agree. Here's to Peggy and her amazing eye for detail! Thank you so much, my friend!

BIANCA D'ARC

PROLOGUE

"**O**h, crap."

Donna Sullivan realized her mistake almost immediately as four big Chinese guys stood up from a table in the rear of the restaurant she'd just entered. All of them were staring at her as they headed her way and they didn't look friendly.

Maybe she'd asked a few too many pointed questions in the wrong places. She was new to all this femme fatale stuff. She'd only been recruited to join a top-secret military team a few weeks ago and then, only by default. She'd earned the dubious honor because she was immune to the contagion that had the country's top scientists and a select group of Special Forces operatives scrambling to not only keep it secret but to contain it before anyone else died.

It looked like Donna had gained the attention of some of the Chinese mobsters she'd been looking for, but in a really bad way. Cursing the tinkling bell over the door, she sprinted out of the restaurant and down the street as fast as her legs would carry her. She had to get away. She wasn't far from the rooms her partner, CIA Agent John Petit, had insisted on renting in a rundown building off Grant Street. Maybe she could get there before those guys caught up with her. Maybe if she just cut through this alley…

Donna ran for the narrow opening, trying to evade pursuit. Those seriously scary guys were definitely following her. A quick glance down the street before she turned into the alley confirmed they were running after her. She took off, looking over her shoulder to check the mouth of the alley when a big hand reached out of nowhere, grabbing her around the waist.

The unknown assailant dragged her into a dark doorway. It shut ominously behind her with a soft click. A hard male body pressed up against her as one big palm covered her mouth and his other arm held her around the middle. Had she gone from the frying pan into the fire?

Pounding feet sounded just beyond the flimsy door. She did her best not to make a sound. The guys who were chasing her were definitely bad guys. She didn't want to betray where she was. She'd rather take her chances with this lone assailant than with the four who had been chasing her. She liked the odds better, even though she was no Chuck Norris. Hell, she wasn't even a Chuck E. Cheese. She had zero combat skills, but she'd go down fighting, regardless of how badly she actually acquitted herself.

"What the hell did you think you were doing?" A tense whisper sounded near her ear. She knew that tone of consternation with an edge of steel.

Thank the good Lord, it was John, her so-called partner in this mess of a mission.

He let go of her mouth as she relaxed into his hold.

"I was trying to get the information you seem so reluctant to go after," she challenged, keeping her voice low.

John let her go completely and started walking into the dark interior of the hallway. He'd dragged her into the little-used alley entrance to their building. She followed him down the short hall, up one flight of stairs, and into their rented rooms.

"Who's the trained agent here?" He turned on her as soon as she'd locked the door behind them.

"Dude. Do not pull that on me." She tugged her shoulder

pack off and plopped it with more force than was necessary on the console table near the door. The place had come with the bare bones of furniture. "I know you were a Marine and some kind of CIA spook, but what do jarheads or spies know about detective work? Your sister at least was a cop before joining this screwed-up team. If she were here, I can just about guarantee that she wouldn't be sitting on her butt twiddling her thumbs, waiting for the information to fall from the sky into her lap."

"You don't know a thing about my sister. And for that matter, you don't know a thing about me either."

She backed down, duly reprimanded. He wasn't saying anything but the truth, no matter how much it might hurt. "You're right. I don't."

He grabbed his knapsack and started gathering the few things he'd left lying around the small apartment. He was packing.

"Go change your shirt and put your hair up. Then get your stuff together. We have to leave."

"What? Why?"

"It won't take them long to figure out where you went. They lost you in the alley. There are only a few places you could have gone from there. They'll check them. All they have to do is talk to the building manager or any of the tenants who've seen you."

She hadn't thought of that. She went into the room she'd been using and tugged off her red T-shirt, replacing it with a blue tank top. "How did you know where to find me?" She raised her voice to be heard as she quickly scraped her hair into a ponytail and donned a baseball cap.

"I was watching the street and saw you run out of the restaurant. You're quick, I'll give you that. I almost didn't catch you in time. I swear, Sullivan, you took ten years off my life."

She raced around the small room, gathering her belongings and stuffing them into her knapsack. She'd packed light for this trip. John had insisted. She was glad of it now, though she'd fought him at the time.

Considering they were now on the run because of her, she thought maybe she should cut John a little slack. He might be autocratic and a total chauvinist, but he was also proving to be right about a lot of things. Damn the man.

"It's okay." She stood in the doorway to her small room, ready to go. "You returned the favor when you grabbed me like that. I thought I'd traded four goons for one possible ax murderer."

He sobered. "You could have." His gaze pinned her, deadly serious.

"Yeah, I see that now. I'm sorry, John."

"Sorry?" He smiled tightly as he checked the windows, then peered through the peephole. "I never thought I'd see the day you'd apologize for your headstrong ways." She would have argued with him about his rather insulting phrasing but she saw his entire body tense. Something was up. "Do you have everything?" His voice was pitched low and tense.

She nodded, slipping her knapsack over her shoulder.

"One of your friends from the alley is in the hall, talking to Mr. Chen." John kept his eye to the peephole. "He just flipped open his cell phone. Calling for reinforcements, I bet." His expression turned steely as he pulled back from the door and turned to her. "Hold this. I'll be right back." He handed her his bag, which was even lighter and smaller than hers, before opening the door. He shot out like a race-horse just released from the starting gate.

She heard muffled thuds through the closed door as she raced toward it. She pressed her eye to the peephole just in time to see one of the big bruisers who'd chased her go down in a heap at John's feet. She knew John was a martial arts teacher of very high rank, but she'd never really seen him in action before.

The guy on the floor hadn't even had time to draw the big gun she now saw he wore under his jacket. John relieved the unconscious goon of both his gun and his wallet, doing a fast, careful search of his pockets while he was at it. When John stood, she opened the door and met his gaze. Gone was the exasperation she usually saw from him. All amusement had fled as well.

The man who looked at her was a hardened warrior. Intellectually, she'd known John was a tough guy. She'd just never seen him like this before. It was impressive, to say the least.

He held out one hand to her and she followed his unspoken summons without thinking. She was at his side in ten steps, holding out his pack to him. He took it, then tugged her hand into his as he turned toward the exit—not the front door, but the door they'd used minutes before. He didn't let go of her hand until they were down the alley and on the opposite street, joining the busy foot traffic prevalent in this part of town.

He let go of her hand only to put his arm around her waist and tuck her into his side. They strolled down the street, just another tourist couple out for a stroll.

"Where are we going?" Donna asked, trying to look nonchalant and no doubt failing.

"The airport. This town is too hot for us right now and I think we've learned all we can here. While you were out stirring up trouble, one of my bugs paid off. I've got a location and a name that matches one of the original research team members."

She was astonished his methods had actually worked. "Really? Who?"

"Dr. Elizabeth Bemkey. She's in Tennessee right now according to what I heard."

He looked like the cat who'd swallowed the canary as he smiled down at her. She squelched the impulse to wipe that silly grin right off his handsome face. The man could be truly infuriating at times.

"So we're going to Tennessee?"

"Looks that way. Ever been fly-fishing?"

CHAPTER 1

They touched down in Tennessee after catching a connecting flight out of Houston. The plane dropped them in Nashville, about an hour and change from their destination. John rented a car and they were off. A straight shot across the state on Interstate 40, then a little trek on a state highway and they were there.

John made good use of the time, placing a few calls and coordinating with the folks back at Fort Bragg, where their team was currently based, while Donna drove. She had a bit of a lead foot, but was competent behind the wheel. They entered White County and turned off at Cookeville, which was a larger city, where they could pick up appropriate clothing and fishing gear at one of the big chain discount stores.

"I'll get some fishing gear while you pick out some clothes," he told Donna when they entered the giant store. "Get stuff for a leisurely vacation by the lake. Make sure you include darker colors for night work and a hat for daytime. If we go out on the water, the sun is going to be tough on your fair skin."

She had looked at him strangely when he made the observation, but thankfully hadn't remarked upon it. John had spent all too much time lately fantasizing about her skin. Was it as soft as it looked? Would she be sensitive to his merest touch?

Damn. He was doing it again. He shook himself and refocused on his task. He needed the bare bones of fishing gear. Just enough to make him look like he really was going fishing. He'd made reservations at a fishing camp that was nearly next door to Dr. Bemkey's palatial home on the lakeshore. It had been her husband's house, and as they'd been going through a very messy divorce for the past year or more, nobody had expected her to be there. They'd sent agents to check, of course, but her husband claimed not to have seen or heard from her in quite some time. Apparently they did all their talking through their lawyers at this point.

But according to the information he'd intercepted in San Francisco, Dr. Bemkey was not only staying in her ex-husband's mansion, she was working from it. It was up to them to confirm the information and figure out what she was up to.

Donna caught up with John while he was trying on vests with a few million pockets for fishing lures and tackle.

"You look like a dork in that." Her dryly amused voice came from behind him.

He turned, holding his arms out so she could get a good look at the ensemble. "You think so?"

"Oh, yeah. If you were going for the Poindexter look, you nailed it." Her luscious lips quirked up in a half grin that he found utterly captivating.

"Question is"—he moved closer, his voice dropping so only she could hear him—"would a young hottie like you be seen cavorting on the lake with a dork like me?" His arms slipped around her waist, but he resisted the urge to pull her against his body. He could get away with just so much in the name of their cover. If he started to grope her in the sporting goods section, it wouldn't be to convince people they were together. No, it would all be for his own enjoyment.

"Cavorting?" Her tone was the slightest bit breathless as

her palms settled over his chest. Damn, that felt good.

"They're a little more old-fashioned here in Tennessee than they were in San Francisco. We'll draw less attention if we show up as a married couple."

"Married?" The word whispered out of her mouth and it was all he could do to stop himself from leaning in and capturing her lips with his own.

"How does Mrs. John Pettigrew sound? Close enough to my real name that it'll be easy to remember?"

Mutely, she nodded. Something weird was going on here. She looked utterly stunned and he was feeling more than a little odd too. He'd never been on an undercover assignment with a female operative before. Certainly not one that required them to pose as lovers. Why did this feel like so much more than a simple mission?

"So what do you say? Is the vest too much?" He stepped back, trying to resolve the weird vibes in the air with a change of subject.

"The camo vest with the camo hat is definitely too much." She flipped through the rack of vests to find something in a solid color. "How about this one?" She held up a solid green vest.

He'd automatically gone for the camo, but she was probably right. The only place he'd be wearing the vest was on the lake itself. He probably wouldn't be traipsing through the woods in it.

"It looks good." He took a quick look at the size she'd picked. It would fit. He threw it in the cart with the stuff she'd picked out. He noticed she'd gotten him some things. "You bought me shirts?"

"And shorts," she confirmed. "If you need to go for a swim, it's best to be prepared." She held up a pair of board shorts that would double as swim trunks should the need arise. They were his size too.

He shot her a suspicious look. "Have you been checking out my ass? You got all my sizes right."

"As if." She flopped the shorts back into her cart. "It's not that hard to differentiate between large and extra large, John," she protested, but he saw the slight flush of color on her fair cheeks and was oddly flattered. "Is this stuff yours too?" She pointed to a pile of gear he'd been toting around. He hadn't gotten a cart. He'd just been carrying the stuff.

"Yeah." He picked up the tackle box and gear, loading it into her cart. "Okay." He took charge of the now stuffed cart as they headed out of the sporting goods section. "Two more departments and we're done."

"Two?" she questioned, walking beside him down the wide aisle of the super store.

"Yeah, I want to get some supplies. A cooler and some food. Snacks, beer, chips. The kind of stuff people would bring for a week at a fishing cabin."

"And the other department?"

"Rings," he said simply. She didn't say another word until they started debating the merits of various kinds of potato chips in the grocery section of the store.

When they finally moved on to the jewelry counter, John picked out two simple gold bands and a petite engagement ring. They were posing as newlyweds of moderate means. The diamond was small, but it still took her breath away when she tried it on. John paid for the rings quietly and stuffed them in his pocket as they left the store.

He let her drive again as they headed for the last leg of their journey while he was busy taking all the tags off their purchases. They stopped at a fast food place on the highway for a quick meal and he got rid of the evidence of their shopping trip, throwing out the bags and tags in the garbage.

"Check out the billboard." John pointed to a big man grinning down at them from a huge advertising board that looked over the fast food joint's parking lot. The twenty-foot-tall image was of a portly man in overalls. He had a big gap between his front teeth as he grinned, holding up a giant fish on a line.

"'Bubba's Bass Tours,'" Donna read from the sign. "'Let Bubba guide you to the best fishing holes in Tennessee. Daily and hourly rates.'" Donna took a sip of her soda. "Now I know we're in the South."

"Did you see the live bait machine near the drive-thru?" His eyes reflected humor.

"The what?"

"The bait machine. Put in a couple of quarters and out pops a plastic container full of wiggling worms."

"You're kidding."

"'Fraid not." He saluted her with his burger before taking another healthy bite.

"I guess there's not much else to do in the area but fish. Seems to be the main occupation of folks around here. Even the guys in line in the fast food place were trading fish stories."

"Yes, ma'am. We're in lake country up here. Too bad we can't enjoy any of the fishing-related activities."

"You like fishing?"

"I used to have a dune permit for my four-wheel drive," he admitted with a hint of pride. "I've been known to cast a line or two of a morning."

"I had a neighbor that was into it. He had plastic tubing mounted on the front of his dune buggy to hold the fishing poles. Don't tell me you've got that kind of setup."

"Once upon a time, I did," he admitted with a chuckle. "I'm a lot more low key nowadays."

"Thank goodness for that."

Donna finished her burger and rolled up the paper it had been wrapped in, shoving it all in the paper bag for easy disposal. John did the same and hopped out of the car to throw out the garbage. A few minutes later, they were on the road again.

She drove again as he snoozed in the passenger seat, his new camo fishing hat pulled over his eyes. She was pleased that he wasn't going all macho on her about the driving. Almost every man she'd dated had insisted on driving everywhere as if she wasn't to be trusted behind the wheel or something. John apparently felt comfortable enough not only to let her drive but to nap while she did it. She liked that about him.

In fact, she liked a lot of things about him. He could be an overbearing, pigheaded fool at times, like most men she knew, but he also had some endearing qualities. His playfulness on their shopping expedition was new and completely attractive. She thought he must finally be getting comfortable with her. It gave her a warm feeling.

She'd sensed his disappointment when she'd been assigned to work with him. He was a man of action, used to being in the field, in combat. She was an albatross around his neck. Or so he'd thought. The foolishness she had committed in San Francisco was at least partly because she had wanted to prove herself to him.

She didn't want to be an albatross. She wanted to be part of the team—a full contributor to their mission. She still wasn't sure what she could contribute. She wasn't a soldier, cop, or top scientist like the rest of the team members but she could learn. She knew how to shoot. She'd had to spend a couple of memorable hours at a firing range with John to prove she could hit a target. He'd seemed impressed, but with John's poker face, it was hard to tell what he was thinking most of the time.

He'd personally approved her to carry a weapon and had trained her in the care and use of the special toxic darts they used to destroy zombies. Years of lab work to earn her master's degree in chemical engineering had helped her get used to the strict protocols necessary for handling such dangerous ammunition.

Despite all her work to this point, if not for her immunity, she would never have been asked to join the team. She knew the truth. She understood that she was seen as the weakest link in the group. Instead of letting it annoy her, as she had in the beginning of this venture, she saw it as a challenge now. She worked extra hard to prove herself and was glad when she got those little signs of approval from her stoic partner.

As she pondered it all, the car rounded a curve on the

mountain road and Donna suddenly beheld the most amazing sight she'd ever seen through a car window.

"Holy moly," she muttered, unable to keep from exclaiming at the sight that met her eyes. They were riding along the side of a mountain, about to turn onto a two-lane road that would take them over the top of a massive hydro-electric dam.

"What is it?" John roused from his nap, plucking the silly fishing hat off his face to look around.

"Sorry. I didn't mean to wake you. I've just never seen anything like this before in person."

"What? The dam?" He looked at her, one tawny eyebrow quirking upward in an amused question mark.

"They don't have these things on Long Island," she grumbled, turning onto the dam itself. To one side was a massive lake that stretched as far as she could see. On the other side was a sheer drop down the side of the dam. She put both hands on the steering wheel, feeling just a little trepidation at riding along the top of such a thing. Only this comparatively thin wall of concrete held back a massive amount of water.

"So you're a city girl?" He sat up and took a look around seeming to enjoy the view.

"Come on. I know you've seen the file they have on me. You know I was born and raised on Long Island."

"Yeah, but hearing about it from you is different than reading it from a piece of paper."

She'd give him that. "I hear from your sister that you two are from the Island too."

John nodded. "We grew up in Lynbrook. But you're a Suffolk County kid, aren't you?"

She hated the way he turned the conversation back to her every time she asked a question about him. "Smithtown. But you already knew that."

He nodded, a smug smile telling her he knew she was miffed. "We're over the dam. You can release your death grip on the steering wheel now." His words were soft.

Almost…understanding?

She looked around and realized they'd crossed over the dam while he had been distracting her with his questions. She consciously released the fingers of one hand from the wheel. He was right, darn it. She had been holding the thing way too hard. Her knuckles were white until she relaxed her fingers.

"Where to now, navigator?" They'd come to the exit he'd told her to look for. She took it and waited at the bottom of a short ramp.

"Make a right. There should be a sign somewhere up ahead for the fishing camp. We've got a cabin reserved for the week. I asked for one on the edge of the property. I told the guy we were newlyweds and wanted a little privacy." He winked at her. "So do your best to look happy when we get there, okay?"

"Don't worry. I took a few acting classes in undergrad. I'm sure I can fake not despising you for a few minutes."

He laughed out loud at her insult. They'd been trading barbs since almost the first day they started working together. It was comfortable for them and had morphed into an odd sort of affection. The more they teased each other, the closer they became.

She found the sign and turned into a wide gravel drive. "This place looks kind of rustic."

There was a main building that advertised itself as both an office and a bait shop. She could see little cabins scattered around through the woods. They were set far enough apart, and the woods were thick enough, to give the illusion of privacy.

"This place borders the Bemkey estate on one side and provides direct access to the lakefront. It's perfect for our purposes."

"Convenient." She pulled up, parking the car to the side of the office door.

John grabbed her hand before she could open her door and get out of the rental car. She looked at him, meeting his all too serious gaze.

"Give me your left hand, Donna."

She caught her breath as he took her hand in his, slipping the gold bands he'd bought—one sporting that small diamond—onto her finger. The atmosphere was charged. The air stilled as they shared the intimate moment. She didn't dare breathe as John moved closer, placing a chaste kiss on her lips. When he pulled back, he was smiling.

"I've never given a girl a ring before. I thought the moment should be marked in some way."

His gaze held hers as he searched her expression. She didn't know what to feel. The mere brush of his lips against hers had knocked her world off its axis. It would take a few minutes to recover.

Movement over John's shoulder made her look away. An old guy in an even sillier fishing hat than John's was grinning at them through the passenger-side window. John followed her gaze. Seeing the man, John opened the door, greeting the older gent with some friendly banter. She knew her face was flushed with embarrassment at being caught like a couple of teenagers necking in her father's car as she got out on the driver's side.

The man was named Murray, she discovered, and he had an accent so thick, she had to listen carefully to figure out what in the world he was saying. John didn't seem to be having the same problem as he went into the office with their garrulous host. Donna followed behind, watching as John signed them in as husband and wife. She accepted Murray's congratulations on their supposed recent nuptials and was glad when John escorted her back outside with a wave to their new friend.

He settled her in the passenger seat and took the wheel for the first time since leaving the airport in Nashville. She realized why a minute later as he deliberately got "lost" looking for their cabin in order to check out the surrounding cabins and learn the layout of the fishing camp.

"There's a little map on the back of the rental agreement," Donna told him as they turned around for the second time on the narrow gravel road.

"I know." He spared her a withering glance as he backed the car into a three-point turn. "It's just easier to see things in person first so I'll be able to judge whether the scale of that so-called map is accurate."

Donna gave up. He knew what he was doing, even if it didn't seem like it to her. "A little communication would go a long way in this relationship, John."

He grinned at her as he started down the gravel road again. "Now you really sound like a wife."

She had to laugh. She'd heard her mother make the same kind of sarcastic observation to her dad all her life. "Yeah, I guess you're right."

"You're right too," he surprised her by saying. "I had some time to think on the plane and as you drove. A lot of our problems in San Francisco were caused by my not telling you what I was doing. Am I right?"

She considered his words and the conciliatory tone he'd spoken them in. It felt like he was extending an olive branch. She'd be a fool not to take it. She really didn't want to fight with him.

"It felt like you weren't doing anything when it turned out you had your reasons, and methods I didn't know about. It felt like I was being kept in the dark."

"Which is entirely my fault." He shook his head once as he concentrated on the road. "My only excuse is that I'm used to working on my own. I don't usually explain myself to anyone. In my current line of work, I can't. Secrecy has become a way of life for me. I'm sorry I didn't fill you in, Donna. You're new to all this and Commander Sykes made a point of asking me to take you under my wing and teach you what I could. I haven't held up my end of that bargain."

She was floored by his admission. "It's okay. I haven't been the easiest person to get along with either. I get a little sarcastic when I feel out of my depth. I've been feeling out of my depth since I woke up in the woods back on Long Island. Actually, even before that, when my boyfriend turned out to be a zombie."

They hadn't talked much about the incident that had brought her to the team of zombie hunters. She'd been doing her best to forget it, but maybe that hadn't been such a good idea after all. She knew she had to deal with the fear and pain of betrayal sooner or later. Especially if she could be confronted by the creatures again.

"How did it happen?" His gentle tone invited confidences.

"I was supposed to meet Tony at the track on the athletic field. He was part of the football team and I was going to meet him after practice. We were supposed to go to a movie, but when I got to the track, nobody was there. I walked around a little, thinking maybe they'd just moved to a different part of the field. I guess I got too close to the strip of woods that bordered one side of the field. I saw Tony there, under the trees, from a distance. It was after dark, so I couldn't really see him until I got closer. He was standing with a bunch of his friends, so I thought nothing of it when he didn't see me at first. I thought he was talking to his buddies." She paused, her mouth going dry as she remembered what happened next.

"But he and his friends were already dead, weren't they? They'd turned into zombies by the time you found them." John stopped the car in front of the cabin farthest out, along the boundary of the fishing camp. There were woods all around. They reminded her a little of that fateful night.

"It was horrible. They made this moaning sound and their faces had been mutilated. Tony was lucky—he still had most of his face, though he was missing part of an ear and his cheek had been slashed clear through. He was all scratched up and his clothes had been shredded in places." She shuddered remembering the brown stains of dried blood all over the young man who'd been so vital and vibrant.

"You must have loved him a great deal."

The question shocked her out of her gruesome memories. "Love? No. We'd only been dating a week or two. He was a good guy, but he was a year younger than me. I felt like I was getting away with something dating him, but he claimed not to care that I was a cougar." She laughed at the remembered joke. "He had a good sense of humor and he was smart as well as athletic, but I'm not sure we would have worked as a couple long-term."

John's relief at her explanation of the relationship was heartfelt. He'd been worried that she would be scarred by the loss of her boyfriend. The file he had on her gave bare facts. He hadn't been able to figure out if she was heartbroken or merely shell-shocked by the events that had led to her inclusion on the team.

"So what happened next?" He'd shut off the car's engine, but was in no hurry to go inside the cabin. They were getting to the heart of some serious stuff here. He didn't want to spoil the mood until he'd heard as much of the story as she would tell.

"He grabbed me and it felt like he was shielding me from the rest of the team. Hands reached out to claw me, but he folded me in his arms and moved away. He was a really big guy. Bigger than you, even. And strong. He picked me up and carried me off through the woods, his zombie friends following along after." She paused, a frown marring her soft brow. "I don't really know what happened next. I saw a female cop and a guy in camo. They were firing darts and I thought they had to be kidding. I mean, come on, darts? What good would that do? But one by one the guys started disintegrating." Revulsion crossed her expression. "Tony bit me before he succumbed. I'd also been scratched up pretty badly by the others when they tried to grab me away from him. I suppose he was trying to protect me in some way, but in the end, he ended up infecting me with the contagion." She gave a wistful sigh. "I passed out. I don't know for how long. I woke up in the woods just before dawn and made my way to my dorm room. I cleaned up, but I felt horrible so I checked myself into the campus clinic. Shortly thereafter I was approached and offered a position with the team. The rest, you know."

"Yes. Sarah was abducted and all hell broke loose. Nobody had a chance to check on you until much later. But I don't understand why you didn't tell anyone about what had happened to Tony." That had been bothering him. Why hadn't she told anyone about the zombies?

One sleek eyebrow rose in challenge. "You think anyone would have believed me if I'd run to campus security babbling about zombies? They'd have thought I was coming down from an acid trip. I looked like hell. I felt like hell. All I wanted was a nice place to rest and a doctor's opinion on my condition. For all I knew, it could have been a drug-induced hallucination. I certainly felt bad enough afterward. I figured someone could have slipped me something without my knowledge. I don't do drugs, but they're easy enough to get on any college campus. I wanted a little time and perspective to think about what I'd seen before I started talking about zombies. I didn't want to be committed to a psych ward somewhere with padded walls." She laughed but he saw the wariness in her eyes.

"That was probably good thinking on your part," he admitted. "It certainly helped the team keep a lid on the operation on Long Island. I didn't find out about it until well after the fact and my own sister was involved." He still couldn't believe his baby sister had become mixed up in something so dangerous and covert.

"I like your sister. She seems like a gutsy woman."

"Gutsy enough to become a county cop in the face of our dad's disapproval," he agreed. "I have to admit, even I wasn't entirely comfortable with her choice of profession. I was raised to believe the man did the protecting and the woman did the nurturing."

"Why can't both sexes do both?" she challenged him. That was something he was coming to really enjoy about their exchanges. "After all, even in the most basic terms, the female is always involved in protecting the young as well as nurturing. And men have always been teachers of the next generation. That's nurturing in my book."

"Good point, but you don't know my dad. He's formidable and, in his little world, his daughter becoming a cop was a sacrilege. I like to think he's come to terms with it by now, but I'm not sure. I know I had a rude awakening when I found out Sarah was part of the top-secret covert team I'd been invited to join. Hell, my little sister is the reason I got this gig." He had to laugh. "It was a shocker."

"I bet." She looked amused at his expense but he didn't really mind.

He opened the car door. Their intimate talk was over and it was time to go back to work. They worked well together over the next twenty minutes, quietly moving into the small, rustic cabin. He left her organizing their food supplies while he did a circuit of the woods surrounding their cabin before it got too dark to see.

They were well situated—on the border of the Bemkey estate's lands and close to the lakeshore. The nearest cabins were somewhat visible through the trees but far enough away to give them a lot of privacy. The woods provided a natural screen that shielded their cabin from easy view of the others. It was the perfect setup to do some quiet surveillance of the estate next door.

When he was satisfied they were secure, he returned to their cabin. Donna was waiting for him on the small front porch.

"Is it okay to walk down to the lake? After all that driving, I need to stretch my legs."

John thought about it, looking around. They were reasonably close to the lake. He could see the water's edge through the trees from the cabin's porch.

"It should be okay. Don't venture too far into the woods, just in case. I haven't gotten any reports of missing people in the area, but if Dr. Bemkey really is in residence and doing research here, you never know what could be hiding in the woods."

She shivered, rubbing her arms. "I'll stick to the lakeshore.

I just want to walk a bit. I won't be more than ten or fifteen minutes."

"Fair enough." John nodded at her as she passed him going down the stairs to the dirt path leading to the lake. "I'm going to check in with base and fire up the laptop."

"See you in a little bit." She waved over her shoulder as she headed toward the lake.

Sunset was just beginning over one side of the lake, casting a rosy glow over the water. It really was beautiful. John watched her progress out the front windows of the cabin as he puttered around inside. Every few minutes he looked out to see how she was doing. He couldn't help it. He was protective of her. Maybe even a little overprotective. It was part of his nature and upbringing to protect women, even those who could take care of themselves.

She'd held up well so far. Even after the fiasco in San Francisco, she'd bounced back better than he'd expected. She realized she'd made the wrong move there and learned from her mistakes. He'd done a lot of stupid things as a young Marine and even on his first few ops for the agency. The critical thing was that she'd learned from the experience. He could work with that.

He made the call to their team leader, Commander Matt Sykes, at Fort Bragg. They talked for a few minutes about the setup in Tennessee and the situation at Fort Bragg, then ended the call with a promise to report immediately should anything change. John peered out the window to see Donna skipping stones on the mirrored surface of the calm lake. She was pretty good at it too.

Satisfied that she was okay, he powered up the laptop and settled by the front window to do more research into local police reports and newspapers. Missing persons reports would be a good start. They could be an indicator that Dr. Bemkey was up to her old tricks, but so far he hadn't found anything suspicious.

Night fell in earnest while he worked. He heard a commotion and looked out the window to find Donna struggling with someone—or something—down by the lake. It had her by the arm, but even as he rose from his chair, she broke free using one of the martial arts moves he'd taught her. She ran. From the way the being pursued her with a disturbingly lurching gait, he assumed the worst.

The zombies had found them.

CHAPTER 2

John dove for the small locker that contained their weapons and the special toxic darts. Working fast, he unlocked the case, threw open the lid, and grabbed a pistol and two clips, loading the specially made handgun even as he ran for the door.

He was out in the woods before Donna had made it halfway to the cabin. The creature was about half that distance behind her. John passed her, firing on the run, being sure not to get too close. Even a scratch from that creature could mean his death.

"How many?" he asked when he realized Donna had stopped and stood just behind him, breathing hard.

"Just the one." She gulped in air as he scanned the woods. "One minute I was watching the sunset, the next that guy was next to me. Moaning." He saw her shiver out of the corner of his eye.

John walked backwards as the zombie kept coming at them through the woods.

"Keep an eye out behind us. I don't want to get boxed in if there are more of them hiding in the trees." He heard her gasp as she realized they were now alone in the darkening woods with at least one zombie on their trail. They both knew that where there was one, there very well could be more.

"I don't see anything." She was whispering, keeping pace with him as he walked backwards. He could feel her body heat against his back, though they touched only occasionally. She was facing forward, toward the cabin, watching their path while he followed, watching the zombie that continued to stalk them.

"He should be crumbling any minute if what they say is true." He backed onto the porch as the zombie drew closer, following them right up to the cabin.

"They?"

"The guys back at Bragg. I got detailed briefings and simulations, but I've never faced one of these creatures in the flesh before. I wasn't supposed to. They put me on research, remember?"

He grinned, glancing back to catch the dismay written all over her face. Damn. Maybe he shouldn't have reminded her that he wasn't the immune one on this team. He opened his mouth to say more, but the zombie chose that very moment to crumble in front of them.

It was a weird sort of end. He'd heard about it, of course, but nothing could really prepare a person for seeing a human being—or what had once been a human being—dissolve before his very eyes. The guy sort of imploded, starting at the sites where the darts had hit home, until all that was left was a small pile of rags and something that looked like slime.

He heard Donna gasp as the zombie became goo. After checking the woods visually a final time, he turned to her.

"Come here." John tugged her shaking body into his arms. "It's over now, sweetheart. You're safe." She clung to him, her slim fingers fisting in the fabric that covered his chest. He didn't mind. She was shaking like a leaf. He needed to comfort her. It was an imperative in his soul.

His head dipped lower as he nuzzled her soft hair. She lifted her face to meet his gaze and he was lost. He had to taste her. That little teasing peck in the car had cost him deeply. He hadn't stopped thinking about kissing her for real. Taking it deeper, learning her flavor, and what made her sigh in pleasure.

He lowered his head, capturing her lips with his. Yes. This was what he wanted. He pushed his tongue inward and she opened for him as if it was the most natural thing in the world. She tasted of rising passion, a hint of residual fear, and something that made him yearn for more. He'd never get enough of her.

But he couldn't do this. Not really. His life was lived fast and loose. No strings. Ever.

This girl could be a major entanglement. She had complication written all over her. Still, she was sweet to kiss and fit in his arms like she'd been made to belong there.

It was okay to offer her comfort. If he got a rise in his Levi's out of the deal, no harm done. He could help her forget the trauma of the last few minutes and taste the forbidden fruit of her luscious young body while he was at it. He wouldn't let it go too far. A few kisses was all he'd allow. That's all he *could* allow.

A few more minutes of her soft, yielding body against his. That's all he could take. Then he'd let her go and never touch her again. It was better for her. Better for his peace of mind too. Donna was too young for him, too innocent. He'd seen too much of the seamy side of life. He'd done too much. Killed too many people. He was no good for her. Never would be.

He let her go by slow degrees, pulling his lips from hers with great difficulty. Damn, she was sweet. He could almost taste the innocence of her. It was a dangerous flavor. Nothing for him to mess with. He could only tarnish her beauty.

He looked down at her, taking a few moments to gaze into her eyes. It would be the last time he saw that glazed look on her face if he had any willpower at all.

"We'd better go inside, patch you up, and call the cavalry." The change of subject worked. She looked down at herself and the deep scratches on her arm in dawning horror.

"Oh my God, John. You shouldn't have touched me. I need to decontaminate everything." She looked at him with wide, terrified eyes. "I bled all over you. Take off your shirt."

"Now that's what I like to hear." He gave her a wink to lighten the mood as he unbuttoned his shirt. "I'll strip for you anytime, baby."

"Be serious. This could be really bad, John. Go inside and get the decon kit. It's in the red bag. Don't touch anything else. Just get that and come right back out. I'll decontaminate you, then do the rest while you call for a real decontamination team."

"Yeah." He looked around at the remains. "I guess we're going to need a decon team all our own if this is any indication."

He loped into the cabin and spotted the red bag. He picked it up with two fingers and returned to the porch as ordered. It amused him, the way she'd taken charge. He knew she'd been trained in proper decontamination protocol. She had a science background, so he guessed the procedures hadn't been too hard for her to pick up. He'd had a rudimentary course in the same stuff, but he wasn't immune and he wasn't part of a combat or decon team, so he hadn't really paid much attention.

"Open the bag and spill the contents onto this chair." She pointed to one of the plastic patio chairs that graced their tiny front porch. He did as she asked and stepped back as she decontaminated her hands first, using two of the wipes that had been supplied in abundance. She disposed of the specially prepared wipes, putting them in a neat pile to deal with later, then turned to him. "Some of my blood seeped through your shirt. Let me just wipe the area. Hold out your right arm, please."

He did as ordered, trying not to laugh when she started at his ribs and worked her way upward. Few people in the world knew he was ticklish.

"Sorry. I know this is cold. It's the alcohol base in the cleaning solution." She looked up at him as she worked, touching his bare chest and arm with her delicate fingers. It was all he could do to not tug her back into his arms and finish what they'd started.

She was done before he lost total control, thank goodness.

"Could you start a fire in the fireplace? I need to burn these wipes when I'm done and your shirt. And my clothes." She looked at her torn blouse with distaste as she stepped back, out of his personal space. "I can check the remains for I.D.," she offered.

"Only if it won't put you at risk, Donna." He was adamant on that point.

She shrugged. "I'm immune. Hell, the first time, I woke up in a pile of goo. I don't think the remains can hurt me. But I'll be careful to decontaminate everything before I bring anything inside. Because this could really hurt you, John. Hurt as in kill you dead and turn you into one of them. I won't let that happen if I can help it, so you follow my orders when it comes to decon, okay?"

He gave her a jaunty salute. "Yes, ma'am. I like it when you go all militant on me."

She laughed, as he'd intended, and he left her on the porch while he got the fire going and called in the incident to their base. He kept one eye on her the whole time, wary in case there were more of the creatures out there. She'd done well tonight, but she'd gotten injured. He didn't like that at all. The deep gouges in her arm pained him to look at, yet she carried on, doing her job and not complaining. She had more grit than he'd thought. She soldiered on when she had to, which was important. The more he got to know her, the more he found to admire in her character. Not only was she beautiful, she was smart and brave too.

John's eyes almost bugged out of his head when she stripped down to her underwear right there on the porch. Her bra-and-panty set covered her reasonably well, but the sight of all that bare skin sent his pulse into overdrive. She was even more gorgeous than he'd imagined. Full breasts, a tiny waist, and the most delectable ass he'd ever seen. Damn.

She'd been hiding that figure under loose clothing. He'd known she was fit, but her body was that of a goddess. At least to him. He'd always been an ass man and hers was about as perfect as it could get.

She carried the bundle of used wipes into the room, going straight to the fireplace. The blaze was going really well and she wasted no time placing the used white squares on the fire. They went up in little blazes of blue-green flame, powered by the alcohol and whatever other chemicals were in the wipes. He'd made sure the chimney was working properly, taking the smoke well away from them to dissipate harmlessly in the dark night sky.

The way he understood it, once the contagion was exposed to high temperature, of a fire in this case, the contagion came apart and could not reconstitute. It was rendered harmless. So burning was the method of choice for getting rid of anything that could possibly be contaminated.

Donna bent over, poking the fire, and John's mouth watered at the view. She straightened and went back out onto the porch before he could make a total fool of himself. Then she came back with his shirt, dumping that onto the fire in small pieces.

"How did you rip that up?" he asked, curious. The shirt had been heavy cotton. He'd have had trouble ripping it. There's no way she could have…unless there was more to this immunity thing than he'd been told.

"There was a small scissors in the decon kit. Thick cotton like this rips pretty easy once you get it started. See?" She held up a bit of the sleeve and tugged on a tear. The fabric made a soft ripping sound as it tore easily for her. "I figured it would be easier to burn this in small sections rather than dumping it all on at once. It could have smothered the fire."

"Good thinking." His mouth was as dry as a desert. Seeing her prance around in her undies had that effect. That effect, and others. He kept the couch between them so she wouldn't see his rather blatant response to her near nudity.

"I found a wallet in the pocket of the man's trousers." Her

words diverted his attention. "I took out his driver's license and something called a 'Frequent Fisher Card' issued from this place. He's a regular. It's got stamps from the last three years, all around this time of year." She headed back to the porch. "I'll wipe the items down as a precaution, then you can have them."

He went to the laptop computer he'd set up by the window. "What was the guy's name?"

"Bill Wallace." She carefully wiped each card and bill that had been in the wallet. He could see her through the open window as she paid strict attention to detail. Her science background was showing. "His business cards say he was an assistant vice president for something called Praxis Air."

John pulled up the man's background information on the computer. "He looks clean as near as I can tell from a quick search," he told her through the window screen. "Poor guy. Probably a bad case of wrong place, wrong time."

"Everything is wet. Don't you think that's odd?" she asked, finishing up. She came back inside and deposited the now clean articles from the wallet on the small table next to the laptop. "It's like the guy went swimming before he decided to hassle me."

"I have no idea what it means. I just hope we won't have a bunch of zombie fish menacing the lake." He chuckled at his own joke.

"It doesn't work that way, from what I've been told. It's human-specific gene altering. It can't cross species. They made sure of it when they designed it. Humans only."

"Lucky us."

"Well, in a way it is. Those zombie fish could cause quite a problem otherwise." She went back out to the porch a final time and brought in the last pile of refuse. The man's remains would stay on the porch until the cleanup team arrived the following day.

Donna squatted before the fire, sending the new stack of used wipes up in flames a few at a time. When she was finished with the used wipes, she took out a few fresh ones and did a final cleansing of her hands and arms, burning those as well.

John settled on the couch behind her, unable to stop himself from looking his fill. She glared at him over her shoulder as she worked.

"Stop staring at my ass," she muttered in warning.

He had to laugh. "How can I help myself when you're prancing around half naked? I'd have to be dead not to notice your smokin' hot bod."

A tingle went down her spine at his words. That hadn't sounded like teasing. His words had been edged with frustration. Had she caused that?

Wow.

Maybe she wasn't the only one having a hard time concentrating with all the bare skin around here. The moment he'd taken off his shirt, her body had begun to purr. The man was gorgeous. He had biceps to die for and the lean, muscular build of a martial artist. She knew he was a highly ranked *sensei*. She'd even participated in a few classes he'd run for the team back at Fort Bragg. But she'd never seen him without his shirt.

Her mouth went dry at the masculine perfection of him. Not too bulky, not too skinny, he was chiseled perfection, like one of those famous marble statues of a young Greek god. She wanted to run her hands all over him and had to clench her fists to keep from reaching out and doing just that.

"I'm covered more than I would be in a bikini," she pointed out, working steadily at the fire.

"For some reason, knowing it's underwear and not swimwear makes a difference. I love the cut of those panties, how they go high up on your hip and make your legs look a mile long." His voice had dropped to intimate tones that sent shivers down her spine. "Of course, right now, I'm sort of wishing you were a thong girl."

"A thong?" She brazened it out, turning to shoot him a daring look over her shoulder. "Do you have any idea how uncomfortable it is to wear butt floss?"

He laughed out loud at her irreverent question, lightening the mood. "Can't say I do. It looks sexy as hell, though."

"Well, it's like walking around with a wedgie all day." She chuckled as she put the last bit on the fire.

"Hold still. I'm dying to know." That's all the warning she got before a warm hand insinuated itself between her skin and the back closure of her bra. She could feel him flipping the fabric over, then tugging on the little pink label that was sewn underneath.

"Ah, it's not a *secret* anymore. Thought so. And may I compliment your taste in lingerie?" Satisfaction laced his voice as he removed his hand from the fabric, skating his warm fingers down her spine.

"John." She tried to object, but it came out too whispery and needful.

"You have a sweet, round, luscious ass, Donna."

That snapped her out of the sensuous spell he'd put her under. "Did you just say I had a fat ass?" She rocked forward on the balls of her feet, out of his reach as she glared at him over her shoulder.

His smile was pure sin. "Round, Donna. Not fat." He sat up on the couch and scooted forward, reaching for her waist only to slide his big hand downward to cup one butt cheek. The warmth began to return. An aroused tingling awoke in the pit of her stomach.

"Round and womanly," he whispered, moving closer. "Perfect." He slid off the couch to kneel behind her. She could feel his hot breath wafting over her back, making her tremble. "The perfect size and shape for my hands." His voice dipped lower as his fingers squeezed. Her traitorous body pushed into his touch. "I've wanted to touch you for days."

Both big hands moved to her ass, squeezing and shaping her flesh. When he slipped one hand beneath the edge of her panties, she couldn't find the breath to stop him.

"A thong would land right about here." His index finger rubbed over her tailbone as his words whispered past her ear, making her shiver. His finger dipped lower, following the valley between her cheeks. He paused only slightly before dipping lower, all the way inside her panties, to cup her mound from behind.

"John," she whispered in warning. His head bent closer to hers, his breath wafting over her ear before his lips captured her earlobe, teeth biting gently. She tilted her head, giving him greater access and implicit permission to do what he wanted. The way he made her feel at the moment, she'd give him anything he asked.

"Yeah, baby. This is what I wanted each and every time I've looked at you," he murmured as he let her earlobe go. "You're wet for me, Donna." His tone was almost chastising as he slid his finger between her lower lips. The tip of his finger teased her distended clit, making her moan. She tried to bite back the sound without success. John Petit lit her on fire with just a touch and she was powerless to resist. She didn't want to resist. She wanted whatever he'd give her, if only for this short space of time.

She knew it couldn't be anything more. John wasn't the kind of man who did long-term. She'd intuited that about him from the very beginning.

She gasped as his finger slid into her without warning, pushing deep. Her body made room for him, accepting him as if he belonged there within her tight core, touching the deepest heart of her pleasure.

"Will you let me, Donna? Will you let me have you?"

She didn't need to think. She didn't want to think. She knew what her answer would be and had known it almost from the moment she'd laid eyes on him.

"Yes."

Things happened fast once the word was out of her mouth. He removed his hand from her panties and turned her toward him, assisting her from her crouch into a much more comfortable kneeling position opposite him. His hands went to her shoulders and down her back, following the line of the silky straps of her bra. He unhooked the catch with deft movements.

"You've done this before," she teased.

He gave her a lopsided grin. "A time or two."

The bra came off slowly, guided by his gentle hands. His eyes followed it as she was revealed to him. She felt a momentary pang of shyness that was quickly smothered as he dipped his head and kissed all ability to reason right out of her mind. His mouth was hot and tangy, his flavor divine, his skill undeniable. He coaxed her tongue into a duel of the most sensuous nature that left her breathless when he finally left her lips, only to trail kisses down her throat.

He licked her nipples, each in turn before selecting one to suck and one to roll between his skilled fingers. She writhed against him as he plied his skills on her willing body. Never had she been so inflamed by a lover's touch, or made so hot by such a simple act.

With John, everything was new and even more exciting. He knew just how to touch her to make her cream. Every time. No exceptions. She'd been in a state of semi-arousal since they had started working together. Since he'd kissed her in the car, she'd been aching for him like she'd never ached for a man before.

He switched things up, licking and nibbling his way across her chest. While his tongue and teeth teased her other nipple, his hands moved downward to cup her ass. He went under the waistband of her panties, pushing them down so he could claim her completely. The fabric fell to her knees as his hands rubbed over her cheeks, and inward as he grasped and lifted. He lifted his mouth from her breast, sucking as he let go with an audible *pop*. He straightened his spine to face her, his arms wrapped around her body, caging her, yet making her feel safe.

"I love this luscious ass, Donna. I can't wait to sink my teeth into you."

"Teeth?" She lifted one eyebrow in question.

"Figure of speech, though I will admit to wanting to lick you all over."

"I think I can live with that." Even if it killed her. Damn, just the idea of what he would do made her want to faint with pleasure.

"I'll make it worth your while, Donna. I promise."

She had no doubts about his intentions. The man was sex personified. Every wicked thought—and she'd had quite a few since teaming up with him—centered on him. John was the epitome of virility in her eyes and there was no question in her mind that he could live up to the advertising of his scrumptious body. This was a man who could deliver.

And it made her shiver to think she'd learn the ultimate truth of that belief any minute now.

"Ready?" His eyes dared her.

"Depends on what you mean?"

"I want to lay you down and begin that licking I was talking about. I warn you, it could take a few days to do properly." The joyful, teasing light hadn't left his eyes and it drew her in.

"Well then." Was that breathless voice hers? "I suppose the sooner we start, the better off we'll be."

"Oh, yeah. And the sooner we can start all over again."

"I'll hold you to that, Romeo."

He chuckled as he lowered her to the soft rug before the fireplace. The flames continued to lick upward into the chimney and gave off a pleasant warmth. She watched the almost mesmerized expression in his eyes as he viewed her naked body.

"How soon she forgets." He shook his head, making a comical *tsk*ing noise. "I'm John. I don't know who this Romeo guy is but, if I do my job right, you won't be able to even think of another man when I'm through with you."

She laughed at his boast. The thing was, she feared he was right. She'd only known John for a few weeks and already every other man she'd ever known faded in comparison to him. She reached upward and twined her fingers around his neck as he moved over her. His eyes met hers and she could've sworn lightning flashed between them.

"Donna, I…"

She stopped him from speaking, placing one finger gently over his lips. She didn't want to hear platitudes, or worse, words he'd spoken to a dozen other girls. She wanted the illusion that this meant as much to him as it did to her. In the bright light of day she couldn't fool herself into thinking a man like John could really be interested in anything serious with a girl like her. But for this moment out of time, she wanted to live the fantasy. She wanted to believe—if only in her own heart—that he could love her, desire her, and want her for longer than a fling.

But if a fling was all she could have with him, she'd take it and be grateful. Men like John Petit didn't saunter into her life every day. Well, not until recently, anyway. He was a man apart. The kind of guy she daydreamed about but had never really believed existed in real life.

And now here she was, living the dream. She wouldn't let anything ruin it. Especially not a few offhand words.

"Come here, John." She pulled his head down so she could kiss him. It was the first move she'd made on her own initiative in this little drama and it felt good. Freeing.

This time, she kissed him. He was panting when she finally let him go and she felt the first stirrings of her feminine power. She smiled, knowing there had to be a wicked glint of satisfaction in her eye. John answered her with a knowing grin of his own before he dipped his head once more, his tongue riding over her collarbone before it slipped downward.

She held on to his shoulders as long as she could while he worshiped her breasts again, lest they forget the way he'd toyed with them minutes before. She writhed under him, her fingers coasting over his muscles as his head drifted downward, his hands leading the way, touching her, testing her, spreading her legs for his passage.

"Look at me, Donna," came the gentle command in John's gravelly voice.

She raised her head a few inches to see him resting on his

stomach between her splayed thighs. His hands were poised over her, as if waiting only for her to watch. Their eyes met for a moment and then he struck.

Callused fingers parted her nether lips, spreading her for his inspection. She quivered as he broke eye contact to look downward at what he'd uncovered. She'd never been this exposed to a lover in her life. A moment of insecurity gave way to a pleasure-filled sense of freedom as he lowered his head, his talented tongue homing in on her exposed clit for a fast swipe that nearly undid her.

"Mmm. You like that, do you?" His words made her squirm as his breath drifted over her skin. "I like it too, sweetheart. You taste like passion and it's all for me." He sounded so self-satisfied she felt a little tingle of amusement snake down her spine. Or maybe it was rapture. John made her feel good in so many ways, it was hard to tell.

"More, John," she whispered daringly.

He grinned at her. "Your wish is my command, baby. This first one is for you."

First one? Did he mean what she thought he meant?

As his mouth settled over her clit and his fingers teased inside her core, she quickly learned the answer to her question. She went off like a rocket with very little provocation, riding John's fingers and mouth like a bucking bronc while he hummed against her, the vibrations going straight to her core.

When she finally began to settle down from the unexpectedly intense climax, she looked downward to meet his gaze. He had a self-satisfied grin on his face that made her want to laugh.

"Ready for more?"

"More?" she panted. "I think I may need a minute to recover."

He laughed outright. "That good, eh?"

"Wipe that smug grin right off your face, Petit."

He only grinned wider. "How can I when you look so cute and flushed and…satisfied? I bet I can make you look even more satisfied, though."

"You're trying to kill me." Her head flopped back on the rug as she closed her eyes.

Wrong move. John must have taken her words as a challenge. A moment later, she felt a light, flickering touch on her clit that stirred renewed interest in places she'd thought wouldn't be up for anything else for a good long while. She lifted her head again to look and saw the tip of his tongue flicking in a move she'd only ever seen once before. And that was in a porn movie she and her friends had watched in freshman year.

Only now did she understand why the woman in the porno flick had writhed like a cat in heat. Within moments, she could have given that actress a real run for her money in the gasping and moaning department. No doubt about it. John Petit knew how to make a woman come. And come again, if he had his wicked way.

"John!" she called out to him as he pushed her pleasure higher. He seemed to take that as a sign to stop what he was doing. Totally *not* what she'd wanted him to do. They'd have to work on their communication skills.

He moved, stalking up her body on hands and knees and she suddenly didn't mind that he'd stopped licking her. He kissed her and she tasted the faint trace of what must have been herself on his lips. It was exciting in a forbidden way.

Her hands stole around his back, enjoying the play of his muscles as she swept downward. She drew up short when she encountered the waistband of his pants. Damn. He still had his pants on. She drew back from his kiss and grasped the waistband, tugging.

"These have got to go."

He pulled back to meet her gaze. "I'm all for it. Want to pull the zipper down with your teeth?"

"I would," she purred, playing along, "but it's a button fly."

They both laughed as he lifted away to kneel between her thighs. His fingers went to the fly and began a slow, sensual display. He unfastened the garment one button at a time. The last barrier between them. She didn't see underwear. He was going commando under those soft cotton fatigue pants.

Hubba hubba.

"Lick your lips like that one more time, baby, and I'll give you something else to lick."

Her gaze rose from his hips to meet his eyes. "Is that a promise?" She licked her lips deliberately, liking the fire in his gaze. It leapt, flaming higher as she watched.

"Next time." He made short work of his pants, pausing only seconds to retrieve something from one of the pockets. It was a square bit of foil. A condom.

Thank goodness one of them was thinking clearly. She reached for it, but he pulled back, tearing the thing open with jagged motions and rolling it over the most magnificent erection she'd ever seen in person. He was long and thick and, suddenly, she didn't want to wait anymore. She wanted him in her. Now.

He appeared to be on the same wavelength. Once he was sheathed and his pants out of the way, he settled between her thighs like a man on a mission.

"Are you ready for me?" He let the fingers of one hand ride through the wetness gathered between her legs for him. All for him.

"Yes," she whispered. "Don't make me wait, John."

"No more waiting." He positioned himself swiftly and slid inside as he lowered over her. He held her gaze as he pushed home, joining them for the first time. If she had her way, it definitely wouldn't be the last.

She was caught up in a whirlwind of sensation as John began to move. He stretched her to her limits, reaching a place inside her on every thrust that made her head reel in pleasure. Damn. He'd found her heretofore missing G-spot without even trying. Now that was talent.

"You're tight, baby. This is so good," John praised her as he settled over her, running his mouth over her neck and shoulder. She loved the feel of him so close to her as he made love to her for the first time. There was nothing stand-offish about John. He was an all-or-nothing sort of man. That carried through to the way he made love, she was pleased to learn.

"John." She couldn't string two words together as her passion rose even higher than before, but she could whimper his name as she rode a crest of intense pleasure. He stroked her higher and higher still as he rode her through her second climax of the day and pushed her toward an unbelievable third.

"That's it, baby." He increased his pace, praising her as he moved more forcefully within her body. She loved the feel of him. The commanding presence and the undeniable skill he had made her insane with bliss. "Come one more time for me, sweetheart. Just once more."

"I…don't know…." She panted, her breath coming in quick gasps as her body soared.

"Do it, Donna. Do it now." It was an order and her body didn't dare refuse. His gaze holding hers, she tipped over the edge into a third glorious orgasm. This one was mightier than the last two combined. She hadn't known she could fly so high or feel so much. She cried out as she came and felt the answering spasms of John's big body inside her.

They'd come together in a rare moment of communion. She'd never had such a powerful simultaneous climax. The thought of it pushed her higher as the pleasure spiraled upward and outward, growing and not diminishing for long, long moments. John held her throughout, fire in his gaze and pleasure washing over them both as they lay entwined, unspeaking.

A long, pleasurable time later, they began to come down from the peak. John smiled his bad-boy smile at her and she answered with a tired lift of her lips.

"Was it good for you?" he asked, the inflection in his voice making her laugh.

"You know the answer to that one." She flexed around him, making them both give a sharp intake of breath as their bodies echoed the pleasure that had claimed them so completely.

"You rocked my world, sweetheart." He rolled with her in his arms, disengaging them as he got to his feet with her held securely in his arms. The man was strong in ways she'd never experienced with another man. Of course, she'd never dated a superhuman sort of ex-soldier before.

He started for the bedroom, a mischievous expression on his handsome face.

"Where are we going?" she asked out of curiosity, though she knew darn well there was a soft mattress in her near future.

"Taking you to bed."

"Bed? Why?" She toyed with the light dusting of hair on his chest, acting coy.

"I told you, Donna. You rocked my world." He paused at the door to the bedroom to look into her eyes. "Let's do it again."

*

In the hour before dawn, Dr. Elizabeth Bemkey looked out from her balcony at the corpses gathered in her backyard. It was marvelous to have them follow her orders. Especially him. The bastard. Her husband and his so-called girlfriend, Claudette.

Lizzie had killed the bastard first with a quick injection to the jugular. She'd enjoyed watching him writhe on the ground, all the while knowing who had brought him death. She'd laughed as he died, holding her gaze. But it wasn't enough. Nothing would ever be enough to repay the pain he'd given her.

She'd stalked the bimbo out on the patio next. Skinny Claudette with her massive breast implants had been easy to surprise. A quick jab to the chest and not only had Claudette been injected with the deadly contagion, but Lizzie had taken great joy in deflating one of the bimbo's boobs a full cup size with aid of the needle and a lovely, spurting, slow leak.

Since then, the other zombies had had their fun with weak little Claudette. She was looking much worse for wear nowadays. The string bikini she'd been wearing when Lizzie had killed her was dirty and torn. Those prize melons had been gnawed by half the zombie population and her once pretty face was pretty no more.

Served the bitch right for stealing Lizzie's husband.

She looked out over her creations, gathered to receive her orders in the backyard. Besides the bastard and the bimbo there was fat Bubba from the infamous Bass Tours, the gardener, and a few odd fishermen who'd been savaged by her pets over the past day or two.

"My little army is growing. Soon, my friends. Soon you will be unleashed on the world." She laughed to herself, the creatures looking up at her with blind devotion.

She liked this change her friend Sellars had engineered in them. Where he'd found the brains to alter the original formula, she didn't know. She never would know now. Last she'd heard, their colleague Dr. Rodriguez had gotten impatient with Sellars and had him killed. Pity that. She would have liked to pick his brain about the improvements he'd already made to the formula. It was her goal to make it even better.

For one thing, she didn't dare go near the creatures. She kept them locked out of the house and only addressed them from up here as a precaution. They seemed docile enough for now, but she wondered when or if they'd tire of following her orders. Still, it didn't matter. They were hers for now and she was enjoying tormenting the bastard and his bimbo especially.

Those two really made her mad. She paced as she fumed, her anger growing. She hated her husband with every last fiber of her being.

"Go jump in the lake!" she yelled down to them. She began to cackle hysterically when they turned and followed her orders, walking slowly in their shuffling gait until they were all fully submerged in the water.

With any luck, they'd stay there until tomorrow night. She had plans for them, but she had to put a few things in place first.

CHAPTER 3

The phone woke John not long after dawn. He wasn't scheduled to check in with base until later in the day. Unscheduled phone calls were never a good sign.

"John, it's Matt Sykes. Things have changed. All hell broke loose here at Fort Bragg last night. I can't spare any personnel to assist you, but we may have another solution. Do you still want in on the combat team?"

"More than ever." John was confused. Matt Sykes had been adamant about not allowing any but immune personnel on the combat side of the team. "But how?"

"Can you two get to Knoxville by oh-nine hundred?"

John did a quick mental calculation. "Yes, sir. I believe we can."

"Good. I'm sending Dr. Daniels to meet you there. She'll explain. And I'm giving you a two-man cleanup team. They should be arriving in Cookeville in a few hours. They'll stay there and commute out when needed."

John didn't need to be told why the cleanup team was positioning themselves in Cookeville. The town was big enough that no one would question their presence. Out in the countryside by the lake, they would probably stick out like a sore thumb. For secrecy's sake, it was better to have them stay in the larger town.

He ended the call with Commander Sykes after being given detailed instructions on where and how to meet Dr. Daniels. John knew Mariana Daniels. They'd been introduced when he joined the team. She was a general practitioner who had been sucked into this mission during the initial infestation at Quantico. She'd been working with the research scientists ever since and John knew her to be a competent professional with a good head on her shoulders. She was also engaged to one of the combat team members, a former Navy SEAL named Simon Blackwell.

When he returned to the bedroom to get his clothes, Donna was awake—just barely. She rubbed her eyes as she blinked against the dappled early morning sun coming in through the window.

"What time is it?" she asked.

"Time to get up." He leaned in to kiss her awake, taking his time but not giving in to the impulse to lay down with her again. If he did that, they'd never get on the road. He straightened and reached for his clothes.

"Did I hear the phone ring?"

"Yeah. It was Commander Sykes. We have to go to Knoxville today. We're meeting Dr. Daniels there at nine."

Donna sat up in the bed, looking adorably rumpled. "Why?"

"He said she would fill us in. Apparently the problems have escalated over at Fort Bragg. They're not going to be able to send us much help, though he did promise a two-man cleanup team would be here sometime today. Dr. Daniels is supposed to explain more when we meet her."

"I don't think I like the sound of that." She shot him a worried look.

He smiled at her, tugging her hand to help her stand. He put his arms around her, settling his hands on the warm skin of her back and that luscious ass of hers.

"It'll be okay."

"If you say so."

He let her rest her head in the crook of his neck for a moment. It felt so good to have her in his arms, he couldn't complain. But time was short. They had to get on the road. Pulling away, he tried to calm her unspoken fears, but only time—and discovering what awaited them in Knoxville— would really solve the problem.

They were able to relax a little on the drive to Knoxville. They made it in plenty of time with a stop for breakfast along the way. Donna was subdued. He could tell she was worried about the unexpected detour to Knoxville. He tried to draw her out as they sat in the waiting room of the VA clinic waiting for Dr. Daniels to arrive.

"What has you tied up in knots, sweetheart?" He took her hand, lacing their fingers together. John liked being able to touch her whenever the mood struck him. After being so careful to keep his hands to himself for the past days, it was a relief.

"I'm not crazy about hospitals and doctor's offices. Even after I woke up in the woods, I thought long and hard before I went to the campus clinic."

"Why? I mean, I don't find hospitals particularly pleasant either, but when you need help, you need help."

"My dad went in for a simple hernia operation a few years back and ended up with a staph infection it took months to cure. They say hospitals are clean, but you can catch some really nasty stuff in them."

He nodded. That explained a lot. He would've said more but Dr. Daniels walked through the door and spotted them. She came over, greeting them both, and taking them back with her into the treatment area.

"They've given me a private room for the day. Longer, if we need it," she explained as they went into a room and she shut the door firmly behind them. She dropped her big briefcase and a cooler bag on a side table and leaned against the bed, facing them. "Here's the deal. Some very bad stuff went down at Fort Bragg last night. Commander Sykes really can't give you any of the immune combat team. He's not being stingy. He really can't spare them right now. Dr. McCormick and I have been running tests on your blood, John. We've been comparing it to your sister's blood. Her natural immunity versus your very close blood match is helping us figure out the way the immune response is triggered. While it's possible you might also prove to be naturally immune, Dr. McCormick and I think we can speed up the process and also make it considerably less painful."

John brightened. "You can make me immune to the contagion?"

If they could manage to do that, his problems would be solved. He could go out in the field and face the zombies head-on. No more pussyfooting around behind the scenes. He could join the combat side of this mission, where he really belonged.

Dr. Daniels nodded slowly. "I believe so. We've done extensive testing and if you're willing, we can do the treatment today. There are some risks, of course. Worst-case scenario, you could die and rise again, at which point, I'd dose you with toxin and you'd end up like the other zombies."

Donna's hand stole into his, squeezing. She was trembling and he knew she was afraid for him. The thought of it touched him deeply.

"What are his chances, Doctor?" Donna asked quietly.

Dr. Daniels looked from their joined hands to Donna's worried face and John knew it was clear they were involved. Oddly, he didn't mind that the doctor knew. He'd have shouted it from the rooftops if he could. The night spent with Donna had changed him. He usually ran when women got the least bit proprietary, yet every second of Donna's concern made him want her more.

"I believe the process will work. I'd estimate he has about a seventy-five-percent chance of walking out of this immune and healthy. There's about a twenty-percent chance that we've made a miscalculation somewhere and he might end up ill, but not in fatal condition. And a five-percent chance of the worst."

"I can live with those odds." John wanted to do this. He felt useless being kept out of the field. The small taste of action he'd gotten when Donna was in trouble had only driven home how badly he wanted to be able to fight these bastards and keep her out of the line of fire, if at all possible. He felt strongly that if his baby sister was immune, he should be too.

Dr. Daniels smiled at him. "I think you can live with them too, John. I would never have suggested this course of treatment if I really thought you'd die from it. Dr. McCormick and I have a strong belief in this and if it works the way we think it will, your experience will also go a long way toward helping our research."

"So he's a human guinea pig?" Donna's tone was challenging. His little vixen had sharp teeth when provoked.

Dr. Daniels sighed. "In a sense, yes. But it's his choice." Her attention turned back to him. "What do you say, John?"

He looked at Donna's worried face and decided to at least pretend to think about it for her sake. "How long will it take?"

"I can administer the shots this morning and monitor you through the process. It shouldn't take more than a few hours. You can probably go back to the lake by tonight. It's likely you'll sleep most of the day while your body adjusts. I'll have to wake you every few hours to take blood samples, but otherwise, it should be relatively painless. We're operating on the theory that a small amount of a watered-down version of the contagion will provoke the immune response in your body. Like a vaccine. Since your blood chemistry is so similar to your sister's and she's already proven immune, we expect you to do well. Just in case, I'll be administering a series of antigens first that we refined from your sister's blood. Since you're the same blood type and genetically very similar, the chance of rejection is incredibly low. We'll wait for them to circulate through your blood, then administer the inactive version of the contagion and monitor your blood for developments. Since this contagion inspires such a rapid reaction, it should be over within a few hours at most."

John turned to Donna. "I want to do this."

"I'm worried," she admitted, breaking his heart with the expression in her beautiful eyes.

"Don't worry, sweetheart." He brushed a stray lock of hair away from her face. "It'll be okay. I have every confidence in Dr. Daniels and Dr. McCormick. If they both agree this will work, who am I to argue?" He gave her a smile, glad when she returned the gesture.

"You trust them with your life?" Her voice dropped to a whisper as she stepped closer to him.

John thought about it and realized he did. "I've researched every member of this team. You know how I love to research." He rolled his eyes, and was pleased when she smiled back faintly. "McCormick is brilliant. She saved one life already with her magic serum."

"But Dr. McCormick was part of the original science team that started this whole nightmare. How can you trust her with your life?" Donna's expression was agonized.

"I wasn't on the team," Dr. Daniels's voice intruded on their moment, but he didn't mind. He could use her help convincing Donna this was the way to go. "I was a general practitioner until I got involved in this. I wouldn't endorse this course of action unless I thought it was the right thing to do. I wouldn't have even come here if I thought this was just another experiment. It's not. Not to Eileen McCormick. And not to me."

"Thanks, Doc. That means a lot." John turned back to Donna. She looked skeptical but better than she had before. He reached down and kissed her lightly, reassuringly, despite the doctor's presence. "It'll be okay. You'll see."

Donna threw her arms around him, hugging him tight for just a few seconds. She drew back and her eyes were suspiciously bright. "If you die on me, I'll haunt you, John Petit."

"Isn't that supposed to be the other way around?" He enjoyed her tough spirit.

"You die on me and I'll change all the rules. See if I don't."

"Then I'll have to be sure not to die, won't I?" One last hug and she let him go. "All right, Doc. Let's do this."

"Okay." The doctor straightened from her leaning position and got to work. "Strip down to your boxers and get on the bed."

"Now that's a sentence a man doesn't hear every day with two pretty women in the room."

Both of the women in question laughed and the serious mood was tempered. He stripped quickly, throwing the clothes at one of the chairs in the room. He didn't complain when Donna—bless her tidy little heart—took each piece and folded it neatly, placing his clothes in the small closet built into one wall.

"We'll start with the antigens and wait a bit for them to spread through your system. If you change your mind after that, no harm done. The point of no return will be after the nonactive contagion is administered."

"Okay, Doc." John got on the bed and held out his arm. "Shoot me up."

Dr. Daniels laughed at his antics and gave him a series of three shots in rapid succession while Donna watched from the foot of the bed.

"How are we doing, John?" Dr. Daniels asked as she took his blood pressure and checked his pulse.

"*We're* just fine and dandy, Doc. What's next?"

"Whoa, tiger." She put his hand on his shoulder when he tried to sit up. "You're staying prone for now. Give the antigens a chance to circulate. If you aren't dizzy in a few minutes, you can stand up and do some stretches to help increase blood flow."

Dr. Daniels stayed in the room, as did Donna, checking his vitals every few minutes and making notes.

"This is getting old, Doc," he groused good-naturedly.

"I'm not used to all this boring inactivity."

"Think of it as the calm before the storm, John. Once we boost your immunity to the next level, you probably won't have another free moment until this is all over."

"Will I gain all those nifty side effects like the super-healing?" The thought occurred to him belatedly.

"We believe so. We're basically re-creating your sister's immune response, only speeding it up."

"Would this work for other people?" Donna asked. "Is this a way to make the contagion work the way it was supposed to? I mean, wasn't the original intent to create something that would boost healing?"

"Unfortunately not. This is a one-shot deal. It'll work on John—and maybe on other members of his close family, now that I think about it. Nobody else." She took his pulse again and stepped back. "You can sit up, but take it slow." He sat up as she observed. "Any dizziness?"

"None," he reported.

Dr. Daniels had him stand and then walk around, each time checking him over before she'd let him do the next thing. Eventually, she sent him back to bed.

"Rest up for a little while. You're making good progress. We'll just wait a few more minutes before we take the next step."

"John, are you sure about this?" Donna couldn't help but ask. The closer he got to taking that final step, the more she worried.

Dr. Daniels looked from Donna to John and back again. "I'm going to step outside. When I come back, I'll confirm your readings and then if you're still prepared to proceed, we'll do the final injection."

"Sounds good, Doc." John watched the doctor leave, then patted the spot next to him where he sat on the edge of the bed, inviting Donna to join him. She walked over and sat down next to him.

John's strong arm slid around her shoulder, drawing her into his side. He felt so good. So warm and stable and strong.

That could all change in the blink of an eye—or in this case, because of a shot in the arm.

"I'm worried."

"I know." He leaned down to nuzzle her hair. "But I'm not. You should take some comfort from that. Despite appearances to the contrary, I'm not cavalier with my own life. It's precious to me and I wouldn't do this if I didn't believe it would be okay. Plus..." He seemed reluctant—almost uncomfortable.

"What?" She turned in his loose embrace to search his eyes. They were troubled.

"My sister was exposed to this contagion. So were you, Donna. I...I feel like this is my chance to be there for you both. If either of you have problems down the road because of this, I want to be there with you—for you. I want you both to know that you are not alone. I see this as a way to help. The more people the scientists have to study, the better their chances of finding a solution."

She read the truth in his eyes. A tear rolled down her cheek, unheeded. She touched his face with trembling hands, brushing his short hair back. "You are the best gift I have ever received in my life, John Petit. I don't want anything to happen to you."

"It won't. Trust me." He winked at her and she had to smile at his unstoppable confidence. If that alone would bring him through the treatment, he had it made.

She wiped her cheek self-consciously. "And here I thought the only reason you wanted to do this was to go out in the woods and shoots zombies."

"Well, there is that." His smile was contagious. "I've felt pretty useless sitting on the sidelines."

"Never that, John. If..." She couldn't bring herself to say it. "I've enjoyed every minute of working with you, John. Of being with you."

He put both arms around her and drew her close. "Ditto, sweetheart."

He captured her lips in a sweet kiss. It was a kiss that

promised more. It wasn't an ending, but a beginning that held hope for times to come. She took heart from his kiss, knowing it was a reflection of the man. He drew back and the feeling remained.

The door opened after a perfunctory knock and Mariana Daniels came back in. John let Donna go and she hopped off the side of the bed, moving to her former position, standing opposite the foot of the bed, against the wall, by the chairs.

Dr. Daniels took her readings and seemed satisfied.

"Moment-of-truth time. Are you still up for this, John?"

"Hit me with it, Doc." He held out his arm eagerly, but his eyes never left Donna's face. Even as the plunger depressed and the dormant contagion entered his bloodstream, his gaze held hers.

The hours that followed were harsh. At first, the contagion didn't seem to have any effect. Then, suddenly, John's muscles began to spasm. It wasn't quite a convulsion, but it wasn't pretty and it couldn't be comfortable. John remained stoic throughout. Between episodes, he began to drift asleep.

"Is that normal?" Donna asked the doctor in a whisper.

"We're charting new territory here, I'm afraid, but his readings are strong and his blood appears to be adapting. Most of the naturally occurring cases of immunity we have seen produced very strong convulsions as the host body adapted. You probably don't remember it because you were unconscious at the time and nobody was around to witness it. Sarah Petit, John's sister, went through it at a hospital and we have very detailed records of her reactions. My fiancé, Simon, had a similar experience, as did the others. Compared to them, these muscle spasms are really nothing."

"Yet you believe he'll have the same immunity and speed healing when he recovers?"

"Yes, I believe so." She'd been taking blood samples throughout the procedure and examining them under a microscope. She also had some other instruments and testing apparatus she'd been using. It looked like she was monitoring the changes almost in real time. "His blood gives every indication of the full immune response. I'll know more when it settles down. The initial reaction is violent with this contagion. After a few hours, it levels out and he should reach his new normal fairly rapidly."

"Do you foresee any long-term problems with the way we are now?" Donna found the courage to ask. She hadn't asked the question before, more interested in the immediate effects. But John's thoughts about the future sparked her own.

"None that I can see." The doctor's words lifted a weight off her shoulders she hadn't known she'd been carrying. "I've done as much research into this as I can because of Simon. We're getting married and he was understandably concerned about his future—about our future. From everything I've seen so far, the new structures in his blood stabilized rapidly and show no signs of deterioration. It's the new normal for him. And for you now. Unless something radical happens, this'll be the way you are for the rest of your lives."

"You almost sound envious." Donna was puzzled by the doctor's reaction.

"I am in a way. You have a lot of advantages. Very little can hurt you permanently now. Including those horrors in the woods." The doctor shivered.

They fell silent for a time, watching John as his body went through another round of spasms. He didn't wake this time and Dr. Daniels monitored him throughout.

"He's a good man, you know." Dr. Daniels removed her stethoscope from her ears and let it dangle around her neck. "And he cares a great deal for you."

"How do you know?"

"It's in the way he looks at you, Donna. The man is smitten." They both laughed at the old-fashioned word. "And you are too. Am I right?"

Donna thought about it. "Yeah, I guess I am. He's not like any other guy I ever dated. He's infuriating and funny and incredibly noble." She took his hand as she stood beside his sleeping form.

"You're in love with him," Dr. Daniels whispered.

Donna wasn't as shocked by the idea as she probably should have been. She hadn't admitted the depth of her feelings, even to herself, but hearing Dr. Daniels say it didn't trouble her. It was true. She loved him. She was in love with John Petit.

How in the world had that happened?

"I can see that's a new concept for you." Dr. Daniels laughed at Donna's expression. She had no doubt she probably looked like a landed fish.

"Yeah," Donna admitted. "I don't know when or how, but I think you're right. Damn." She shook her head and laughed at herself.

CHAPTER 4

John had short moments of lucidity between long bouts of being dead to the world. He was aware of the passage of time only peripherally. They'd started this odyssey around eleven in the morning. By the time he was feeling like himself again, it was closer to dinner than lunch.

"How are you feeling, sleepyhead?" Donna was at his side, holding his hand. He squeezed her fingers, looking up at her beautiful face.

"I'm good." He yawned but the fierce exhaustion that had weighed him down for hours had passed. "What time is it?"

"About four," Dr. Daniels answered from his other side. "Any soreness?"

John tested his limbs as he lay in the bed. "I'm a little stiff, but otherwise okay. I feel like I had a workout, but all I did was sleep, right?"

"Your larger muscle groups spasmed more than a few times," Dr. Daniels informed him. "That's probably why you feel some muscle soreness. How about your joints? Any pain in the knees or elbows? Hands, feet, hips?"

He tested each area as much as he could lying down. "Everything feels okay, Doc."

They went through a lengthy checklist before she would

allow him to even try to sit up. He managed it on the first try, though he had a sensation of lightheadedness for a moment. It quickly passed and as time went on, he began to feel more like his old self. Dr. Daniels took blood samples at intervals, pausing to study the results under her microscope or on one of the other instruments she had set up at the side of the room.

After about a half hour, she finally let him stand up. He was more than ready to waltz right out of there at that point. Only Dr. Daniels's quiet appeals kept him there, answering her seemingly endless questions.

"All right. I think that should do it. Your blood has remained stable for the past three hours," Dr. Daniels informed them. "If it's stable now, it should stay that way. This reaction is a fast one. Your results mirror what we've come to expect and you've confirmed a lot of our hypotheses, John. Thank you."

"So I'm good to go?" He was relieved it was nearly over and he could get out of the desk job and into the field.

Dr. Daniels smiled at him. "You're good to go, John. I know you guys like to patrol at night, but you should probably stay in tonight if you can. You can start your night watches tomorrow night. I don't expect any problems, but if you have discomfort of any kind, give me a call, okay?"

"Yes, ma'am."

John was content to let Donna drive them back to the lake. He dozed off and on, but felt a lot more alert than he had during most of the day. They said little and he sensed Donna was still upset with him. It all came to a head as they drew closer to their destination. He put his hand on her thigh, unsurprised to find her muscles stiff and quivering. She was on edge and he had the disturbing notion that he was the reason.

"Come on, babe. It wasn't that bad."

She glanced at him, and he was shocked to see the brightness of tears in her eyes.

"You didn't have to take the chance with your health, John. I had no choice. I was attacked. You walked into this willingly. Hell, eagerly. I don't understand you. They say we'll be okay, but they really don't have a clue about how this will affect our future."

"Oh, honey, is that what's got you worried?" He tried his best to soothe her. "To be frank, that's why I did it. I meant what I said. I don't want you, or my sister, to go through this alone."

"I bet it didn't hurt that you get to go into the field now and play shoot 'em up with the zombies?" Her tone was accusatory.

"Hell no. I'm a Marine, Donna. My place is in the field. I've trained for combat most of my life. It goes against the grain to have to sit back and watch others fight my battles."

"Especially women?" she challenged.

He took her hand. "Especially you, Donna." His voice dropped to a low tone as he spoke the truth from his heart. "It scares the hell out of me to think of you fighting those things all alone."

"Well, I haven't done a very good job of it so far, have I?" She chuckled brokenly, still fighting the emotion that showed on her pretty face.

"You were never meant to go hand to hand with the bastards. This wasn't supposed to be a mission where we'd go up against them. It was only supposed to be recon. It's not your fault we got way more than we bargained for out here."

"Yet because I can't fight them—and up 'til today I was the only one who could face them without fear—you took a terrible chance with your life and your health."

"You feel guilty?" John was amazed. Nobody had ever taken his worth so seriously before. Well, nobody outside his immediate family. A Marine got used to being one of many. It was disconcerting, and touching, that she thought of him as an individual worth worrying about. "Sweetheart, that's…well, it's flattering. But you have nothing to feel guilty about. Even if I hadn't met you, if I was offered this same opportunity, I would've taken it. Fighting bad things is what I've made my life's work. Being given the opportunity to stop these creatures is an honor I don't take lightly. These things are probably the worst threat to humanity I'll ever come up against. Fighting to preserve innocent lives is what I do. It's who I am."

He'd never articulated his thoughts so well or so wordily before. Belatedly, he was self-conscious about it until he saw the single tear trickle down her cheek. He cupped her cheek, wiping away the moisture with a gentle touch.

"You're a special man, John Petit."

She let it go at that. He moved back and released her hand so she could use both to drive.

"Let's pick up some dinner on our way back so we don't have to cook." He decided a change in subject was in order and he was hungry as hell.

"Good idea. I saw a sign for a chicken place near the turnoff." The atmosphere in the car lightened considerably.

"Sounds good. It's getting too close to dark, or I'd suggest we eat at the restaurant, but I think it's better if we get it to go."

She agreed and they picked up enough food to feed a small army before heading for their cabin.

When they arrived back at the lake, it was clear the cleanup team had come and gone. The tracker and debris were removed from the porch and they'd left a cryptic note to confirm who'd been there. John was glad they'd been discreet. During the day they did see a few people from time to time, though it was isolated out here. Isolated enough that a few zombies running around hadn't been heard and Bill Wallace, the missing fisherman, apparently hadn't been missed yet.

They'd made a quick stop at the office on their way in and John had asked a few subtle questions about Bill Wallace. The owner, Murray, knew the man, but clearly had no idea he was missing, much less that he'd become a zombie. Wallace's reservation had him booked 'til the end of the week. John supposed Murray would find out then that the man had disappeared when he didn't move out of the cabin he'd rented and didn't show up to pay his bill.

"Dr. Bemkey couldn't have been in the area too long or someone would have noticed more missing people by now. Bill Wallace had been attacked," John reasoned as they dug into dinner. "The condition of his face and skin made that clear. So there had to be a primary creature that killed Wallace. And Wallace didn't get here until four days ago. So he had to have been attacked very recently. Within the last three to four days considering he'd need time to rise."

"Can we not talk about that part while I'm trying to eat?" Her tone was clearly teasing and he was glad she'd bounced back from the emotional storm that had gripped her earlier. He wasn't good at dealing with female emotions.

"Sorry. I forgot you had a weak stomach." He stole a chicken wing from her plate and barely missed the fork she swatted halfheartedly in his direction.

"I don't have a weak anything. I'm tough as nails. Ask anyone." The false bravado was as obvious as was the grin on her pretty face.

"Okay, tough guy. Are you up for a little recon in the woods, Marine-style?"

"Is that what they're calling it these days?" She batted her eyelashes at him and he had to laugh out loud.

"My, my. What a one-track mind you have, Little Red Riding Hood. I like it."

"Does that make you the Big Bad Wolf?" She sounded breathless. He felt the tension rise just like that between them.

He set down his fork and swiped at his mouth with the napkin before tossing it aside. He held her gaze as he stood and held out one hand. It was a clear command and she responded as he'd hoped.

She took his hand, her own trembling as she placed her palm against his. He helped her rise from the chair and pulled her into his arms. They came together in a tempestuous kiss, a melding of mouths and hearts and breaths. He couldn't get enough of the feel of her against him, the taste of her against his tongue, the soft scent of her hair in his lungs. She was vital to his continued existence.

"Donna…" He whispered her name as he broke the kiss, only to stroke his hands down her back to cup her incredible ass. Dipping his knees slightly, he lifted her right off her feet, surprising a little yelp from her lips. He liked it. He liked everything about her.

John lifted her onto the countertop in the small kitchenette, urgency riding him.

"Here?" He loved the scandalized note in her voice.

"Yeah, baby. Right here. Right now." He spread her legs and stepped between them. As he'd thought, the small countertop was the perfect height for what he had planned. "That a problem?"

She looked cute as she considered. He could see her thought process written clearly on her beautiful face. Should she get wild with him? Should she let her hair down? Silently, he rooted for her to let go and be daring.

"No. No problem," she said finally, a hint of shyness in her voice. "I've just never done it in a kitchen before."

"Stick with me, babe. I'll take you all kinds of places you've never been before." He crowded against her, nibbling on her lips as she giggled. He liked the sound. It was young, fresh, and sexy, just like her.

He felt like he was getting away with something, having this comparatively innocent young woman in his arms, but he was powerless to resist her. He would take care of her and treat her like a goddess for as long as she'd let him. The future would take care of itself.

"John."

It drove him nuts when she said his name like that. Her breathy, needful voice did things to him. Unexpected things. Things that made him feel…Too much.

"You make me crazy, baby." He breathed the words against her skin as she pushed her clothing off. It wasn't neat and it wasn't orderly, but he wasn't in a very neat and orderly mood at the moment. Judging by her response, she wasn't either.

Within moments, she was mostly naked. All the important parts were uncovered and ready for him. She'd pushed his shirt off and was working on his fly when he had a single moment of clarity and reached into the cargo pocket on his pants for one of the foil squares he had stashed there.

She practically ripped the package out of his hands. She pushed his pants and shorts down over his hips, freeing him.

"Oh, yeah." The words came out of his lips involuntarily as she wrapped her fingers around him, squeezing with exactly the right pressure.

Her other hand brought the foil packet to her mouth. Taking one corner between her teeth, she ripped the wrapper open, allowing the rolled condom to fall. Before it could be lost, she grabbed it, throwing the empty wrapper to the floor instead.

She gave him a tilted smile as she reached downward to roll the rubber over him. She took her time, her light touch driving him higher as she toyed with him deliberately. When the condom was all the way on, she cupped his balls and gave a gentle squeeze. He sucked in a quick breath.

"Like that?" She gave him a blatantly mischievous look.

"You know I do, vixen. But much more of that and I'll start the party without you."

"We can't have that." She removed her hand and he was almost sorry he'd said anything. Then she scooted forward on the counter and put her soft hands around him. It was obvious what she wanted, but he had to hear it from her lips. Her sexy, almost shy way of speaking made him hot every single time he heard that special turned-on tone.

"What do you want, baby? Tell me exactly." She shot him a surprised look.

"You know."

"I won't let you off that easy, sweetheart. I want to hear it." His voice dropped. "Tell me."

A small flush rose up her cheeks. Man, she was something else.

"I want you, John." She moved closer, running her hands over his back as if she couldn't get enough of touching him. "I want you to make love to me. I want you inside me."

He grinned, hearing that perfect tone in her voice. The tone that made his balls ache with need. Yeah, that's what he wanted. He could die a happy man having heard those words from her luscious lips.

"All you had to do was say so, baby." His hands went to her thighs, stroking upward toward the apex between them, rubbing with circular motions as he moved higher and higher until he reached the promised land. The place he would soon possess with an eagerness he hadn't felt since he was a teenager.

He was more than ready to take her, but he had to make sure she was with him. He didn't want to hurt her. He never wanted to hurt her in any way.

"You're nice and wet for me, aren't you?" He met her gaze as he rubbed closer to the opening that wept for his touch. She gasped as he slid one finger inside her. Damn, she was hot. He wouldn't last long. He had to drive her closer to the edge so he took her with him when he blew.

John's finger pressed deep within her, lighting her fire and sending her senses spinning. Then his other hand moved in and those talented, callused fingers found her clit, rubbing in slow circles that sped up as her breathing increased.

"How's that, baby? Are you close?"

"Yes." She threw her head back as her peak neared, closing her eyes as bliss descended on her. Before it could sweep her away, he removed his hands. Her eyes shot open as she searched his expression. He gave her a quick grin as he stepped up, moving into position. "Now, John. Do it now."

John pushed in with little delay. She scooted forward on the countertop to help and they met in the middle. She moaned as he bottomed out within her. Damn, that felt good. No man had ever fit her like John did.

He began to move almost immediately, his big hands anchoring her on the edge of the countertop. Without his support, she probably would have tumbled from her precarious perch, but John was big and strong. His body blocked her from the front and his muscular arms bracketed her. She felt safe and protected…and well loved, if only in a physical sense.

The way he protected her and his gentle touch made her almost dare to hope there was some emotional component in their relationship, but she couldn't be absolutely sure. John wasn't one for discussing his emotions and she didn't dare bring up the subject. Their relationship—if that was the right word for this crazy fling—was too new to test with such a weighty topic.

"Won't be long," he warned her, panting as he sped up his pace. She moved with him as best she could in her position, adding counterpoint that drove them both higher. He was right. It wouldn't be long. She was so close to rapture she could taste it.

"John!" She cried out his name as she came hard, a series of spasms rocketing though her body. His hands gripped her, fingers tightening hard enough to leave bruises, but she didn't care. His strength only added to her pleasure as she heard his harsh groan and felt his body join hers in bliss.

Long moments later, John disengaged and lifted her into his arms. She was half asleep as he carried her into the bedroom and deposited her on the bed. She thought she felt him kiss her brow as he tucked her beneath the blanket.

CHAPTER 5

Donna was sound asleep in his arms when night fell in earnest. She'd had a long day of worry and travel. He decided to let her sleep as he slid out of bed and suited up for a quick look around the woods. Now that he'd been cleared to join the combat team, he wanted to get a bead on the area, strategizing in his mind the most likely avenues of attack and places to hide. He had to see the surrounding forest at night. The way the enemy would see it.

Now was his chance. And if he ran into one of the zombies while he was out, so much the better. He'd take it out before it could threaten anyone else. Donna would be safe enough in the cabin. John wouldn't go far. He'd left her a weapon and locked her securely inside. She'd be okay until he got back.

John headed down to the lake first. That would be his point of reference. The moon had risen over one side of the haunted lake. A thick blanket of fog lay on the surface, like smoke rising from the water. It rippled as a precocious wind tickled the surface here and there.

"That's certainly creepy enough," John muttered under his breath, taking a moment to appreciate the full effect.

He dismissed the strange weather from his mind as he

turned back to locate the cabin through the trees. He'd left a night-light on in the front room, and with that faint glow as his guide, it was easy to spot their temporary home away from home.

Triangulating from the cabin and the lake toward the boundary with the Bemkey estate, John did a thorough walk-through of the woods. He'd done it before in daylight, but everything looked different at night. Somewhat to his disappointment, he didn't come across any zombies. For whatever reason, there was none to be found in the area at that moment.

Deciding he'd been gone long enough, John went back to the cabin and let himself in. Donna was still asleep when he slid back into bed next to her warm body. She had the softest skin. He remembered stroking her hair and shoulder for a while before sleep claimed him again.

Something woke Donna in the middle of the night. For a moment, she was surprised by the warm, hard body in the bed next to her. Then she remembered the night before with John. She could feel her cheeks heat in the cool night air as a little thrill of memory shivered through her body.

It turned to something else when she realized what had woken her. She heard something. Outside.

Tip-toeing out of the bed, Donna went to the window to see what she could out in the darkness under the trees.

She gasped. A zombie faced her, not five feet from her window. Then she recognized the sound. It was that inhuman moaning sound that had woken her, growing nearer the cabin. She froze for a split second before her brain kicked in.

She jumped back from the window and turned to the bed to wake John, but he was already up. He had two pistols in his hands and was loading them with the special dart ammunition. She hadn't even heard him get out of the bed.

"Here." He handed her one of the pistols and she took it automatically.

She was becoming more comfortable with the pistol the

more she handled it. She'd shot rifles with her father and other weapons from time to time but never something like this. Luckily, she'd proven herself a decent shot when they'd tested, then trained her back at the base.

"Guard the door. I'll take care of this and then we'll go together to check the rest. Dress if you can. Shoes are most important." John stepped in front of her as he spoke in a rapid, urgent voice. He wore only his boxers and partially laced boots. He raised the window sash enough to get the barrel of the pistol out and began to fire.

After hitting the creature with four darts in rapid succession, he turned back to her. She'd tugged on her T-shirt and sneakers in record time.

"What now?" she asked, her voice noticeably shaky despite her best attempts to pretend she was as calm as he was under fire.

"We check the rest of the windows first. See if we can get them—if there are more—from here before we go out in the open." He opened the door and eased in front of her, striding boldly forward, checking each window.

When they reached the main room of the cabin, he went to the largest window and sent her to the smaller side windows with a pointed glance. She caught her breath as she noticed two more zombies emerging from the woods about ten yards away. She looked at John for guidance, but he was already firing out his partially open window. She followed his example.

Reaching out with trembling hands, she raised the window sash, fumbling only a little. She sank down and took aim, firing as quickly as she could. They were getting too close.

"Split up your shots if you can," John instructed. "Four shots in each and spread them around."

"Got it." She was proud when her voice only quavered a little. She set to work, doing her best to make every dart count. She had just plugged two darts in each of her targets when another started walking toward the cabin through the woods. "John, there's another one." She heard the fear in her own voice.

"I see him." Their windows were at ninety-degree angles to one another. John was firing at multiple targets, but she didn't dare spare a glance to see how many. She had enough work cut out for herself with the two she was working on and the third on the way.

She gave each of the first two one more round each. She had two more darts in the clip. Should she use the last two darts in the clip for the first two zombies or try to get them into the other one? The moment of indecision cost her. All three were getting closer.

"Four in each, babe. Finish off the first two and we'll work on the third together." John took the decision out of her hands and she was thankful. She followed his directions thankfully.

"I need to reload." She was still breathing rapidly, but John's steady presence helped her focus.

"Catch." He tossed her a fresh clip and only then did she realize he'd clutched a few spares in one of his hands.

It took her longer to reload than John. She wasn't a marksman like him, but she managed. When she looked up again, the third creature was nearly to the front porch. Her racing pulse spiked up a notch. The other two were gone. Thank heaven. She hadn't seen them fall, but there was no other explanation for where they might've gone. She'd hit them with the toxin from far enough away that there'd been time for the toxin to work.

Not so with the third zombie. He didn't even have one dart sticking out of him yet and he was altogether too close if she was any judge.

"John?" He must've heard the fear in her voice.

"Hang in there, baby. I'm almost done with these five. We'll get the other one together, just like I promised, but we need to get the rest under control first or we'll be totally overrun before we can blink."

She fired as he talked and hit the third zombie twice in rapid succession. The shots weren't too widely spaced, but she'd do better. She had to do better. From what she'd been told, spacing the shots out around the torso and legs helped spread the toxin faster. At least, that was the theory. She'd hit her target twice near the left shoulder. It would take awhile for it to spread from there and she needed at least another two darts in the thing before there would be enough of the toxin to take it down.

"John." His name dragged out as she fired another round, hitting the creature in the stomach this time. Better.

The creature veered off, away from her. She couldn't get another shot. "John, he's—" She looked toward him, but he was gone and the front door stood ajar. "Oh, no!" She ran toward the door only to find John facing down the zombie, darting him from point-blank range.

The zombie swiped at him, advancing on John. It was a hell of a sight. John wore only half-laced combat boots and a pair of bright white boxers. He walked backward as the zombie advanced, staying a foot ahead of the ugly yellow claws that had once been fingernails.

Donna scanned the trees behind him, but thankfully there were no more of the creatures. At least none that she could see from her vantage point. She stepped onto the porch and perched at the edge of the top stair. John had led the creature away from the cabin a few feet, off the main dirt pathway that led to the lake and into the grass that bordered the tree line. John walked backward, a step at a time, keeping a vigilant eye on the zombie as it followed his lead.

"Stay back, Donna," he ordered. "Stay on the porch in case there are more of them. This guy should be going down any minute now."

"Be careful, John." She dared not talk above a low whisper.

Her warning came a moment too late. As if in slow motion, she saw John's loose bootlace get caught on a fallen branch, tripping him up. He fell hard on his ass and the zombie bent over him, clawing his chest as John scrambled to recover.

"John!" She came down off the porch, raising her pistol but she didn't dare fire until she had a clear shot. She couldn't take the chance of hitting John. Besides, the thing already had the required four darts sticking out of his gray flesh. Shooting him with another dart wouldn't do any good. The toxin still required a certain amount of time to work.

The zombie appeared to be winning. As she ran toward the struggling pair on the ground, she saw that the creature had John pinned. Her heart in her throat, she tried to think of a way to help. The monster had been a big man in life. He easily weighed twice what she did. There was no way she could pull him off John, but she had to try.

Just as she approached to give what little help she could, John pulled his knees up for leverage and rolled, throwing the zombie off him.

A second later, it dissolved on the ground, leaving behind a pile of ruined clothes and a sticky residue. John lay on the ground nearby, catching his breath for just a second before he climbed to his feet. He had slashes diagonally down one side of his chest that were bleeding, but not heavily, much to her relief.

"Are you hurt anywhere else?" she asked quickly.

"Just my wounded pride. Damn, my butt hurts." He dusted off his now dirt-stained boxers and gave her a rueful, lopsided grin. "Get up on the porch and keep a lookout while I do a sweep of the area. It's close to dawn. Chances are they're going to ground for the day."

"What about your chest?"

He dismissed her question with a shake of his head. "It's not bad." He ran one dirty finger over his chest near the quickly closing gashes. "Son of a gun. I heal fast now. Guess that answers the question about whether the immunity treatment worked." That lopsided grin was back, stronger than before. "Get up there now. I'll be back in a few minutes. Stay sharp. Just don't shoot me when I come back. I'm the one with the white flag on my ass."

He pointed to his boxers and she had to admire his

humor. Grace under fire was this man's middle name. He took a moment to secure his trailing bootlaces so they wouldn't trip him up again and set off silently around the perimeter of the building, his pistol leading the way.

Donna waited for him on the porch, fear in every breath. The sky was beginning to lighten, which gave her hope. So far, the creatures had shunned daylight. When the sun came out, they should be safe.

He came back, making more noise than he usually did. He probably knew she was still jumpy and was making certain she wasn't going to shoot him accidentally.

"Clear," he called softly through the grayness of predawn as he approached the cabin. His steps were calm, yet smooth and rapid. He mounted the small staircase and reached for her arm. "You okay?"

She looked upward to meet his concerned gaze and nodded. "Are they gone?"

"Yeah. Either that was all of them or the dawn scared away any others that were with them. We should be okay now."

She led the way back into the cabin. He locked the door behind them and followed her to the small kitchen area. She dampened some paper towels and turned to swipe gently at the stripes of blood on his chest. The blood was all that was left of the gashes. Not even a red line hinted that he'd been clawed. His skin had healed completely in the short time since the attack. Even though she'd seen similar speed-healing on her own body, she was still taken aback by it.

She said nothing as she bathed his chest, washing away the blood. When he was clean, she stepped into his open arms, needing the hug he so freely gave.

"I'm such a wimp." She hiccupped once as she buried her face in the crook of his neck.

He burst out laughing.

"Sorry." He bit back his laughter. "You are the most un-wimpy woman I know, Donna."

"Yeah, right. Any woman on the team is way braver than

me."

"They're all pretty formidable, but you're no slouch, Donna. I've fought at your side. I know."

She drew away from him to meet his gaze. "If you say so. I think you're just being nice. But I will admit I'm getting a little better. I only froze for a few seconds before."

"You did good, sweetheart. You took out your targets and followed direction. You're a good little soldier."

She chuckled at his teasing tone, but his words and the look in his eyes made her feel better. She reached up and wove her fingers through his hair, coaxing his head downward. Their lips joined. She may have initiated the kiss, but John deepened it, making it grow from something innocent and light to something hot and molten. When he finally lifted his head, she was breathless.

"Come on." He tugged on her hand as he led her toward the bedroom. "I doubt we'll be able to go back to sleep after that, but it's worth a try."

"Are you sure we're safe?"

He looked out the window. "It's dawn. They're gone." He snagged his phone out of his shirt pocket as they entered the bedroom. He'd left it hanging over a chair back earlier. "I should call in the cleanup guys. It'll take them the better part of an hour to get here. I should also report the increased activity to Commander Sykes. It won't take long."

He kept her hand in his as he sat on the edge of the bed and hit the speed-dial with one hand. He spent less than a minute on the line with the cleanup guys, then disconnected and hit another speed-dial button. This time, the call connected with Matt Sykes, back at the base in North Carolina.

She sat next to him as he talked, unabashedly listening in and letting his warmth calm her more. It wasn't every day she faced zombies and shot them down. Nothing had been normal since her boyfriend had become one of them and savaged her.

It sounded like Sykes still couldn't spare anyone to help

them, but John assured him they had the situation under control. She wasn't so sure, but she knew if anyone could handle himself in a crisis, it was John. She'd do her best to hold up her end of the deal, though she wasn't as highly trained.

John ended the call after a few minutes and tossed the phone onto the bedside table. He scooted onto the bed and he pulled her into his arms, spooning her from behind.

"You okay now?" His hands wrapped around her middle, he spoke in a low voice, next to her ear.

"I'm good," she said softly. "You were great out there tonight, John."

"Don't forget your part. You were a big help, babe. I was glad you were there to watch my back."

"You're just saying that." She rolled over to look into his eyes as they lay facing each other.

"I'm not." He raised one hand to cup her cheek, moving eventually to gently stroke her hair back from her face. "I think you're gorgeous and smart and funny. And very capable. You were a big help, Donna."

She didn't know how to respond to the honesty she read in his gaze, so she closed the distance and kissed him. He responded so well, it encouraged her to be more aggressive than usual. She pushed on his shoulder, urging him to lie on his back beneath her. She straddled him, holding his gaze as she tugged her T-shirt off over her head. She was naked beneath and she read the appreciation in his eyes as she knelt over him.

"You hunt zombies in nothing but a T-shirt?" he teased. "Man, when you go commando, you really go commando."

"Well, I had my sneakers on too." She glanced toward where she'd kicked off her shoes when she'd come back into the bedroom.

His hips rose and jostled her higher, but it was worth the momentary fear of falling when his shorts disappeared from between them. His hands reappeared from behind her after completing the task and he wrapped his warm fingers around her waist, just over her hips. She liked the secure feel of his heavy hands anchoring her to him.

"Now we're even." He smiled at her in that devilish way that promised hours of pleasure. She couldn't wait.

"Oh, I like that." She bent over him to place little kisses along his strong jaw. Her hair fell forward to cocoon them in intimacy. "As much as I like you," she dared to whisper near his ear. It was as close as she could come to admitting the growing feelings she had for him. She'd tried to convince herself this was a temporary arrangement. She'd tried to keep it light and she'd failed miserably.

Facing danger with him and fighting at his side had made her feel closer to him in a shorter amount of time than anyone she'd ever known. He'd saved her in San Francisco. He'd saved her again here in Tennessee. Twice. No doubt he'd do it again before this was all over.

She admired his skills. She loved his sense of honor. And she couldn't resist his easy charm. John was all she'd ever looked for in a man and didn't think she'd find.

And she couldn't have him. Not to keep. He had "love 'em and leave 'em" written all over him. She'd known that from the start and she still hadn't been able to protect her heart. She was very much afraid she'd already surrendered her heart to him, lock, stock, and barrel. It was too late to stop herself from loving him now.

But she'd never let him know. That would only send him running for the hills. She wanted to enjoy this while it lasted. She'd deal with the heartache later. Somehow. For now, she had him exactly where she wanted him.

"Where are the condoms?" she whispered in his ear, liking the way his muscles tensed under her thighs.

"Right cargo pocket of my pants." The growl in his voice set her on fire. She looked around the bedroom to see if she could spot the pants. There they were. Flung over the chair next to the bed. Thank goodness.

Donna stretched and nabbed the pants while John placed one of his hands over her breast and squeezed, making her shiver in delight. His action drew her gaze as she pulled one of the dozen foil packets out of his pocket and threw the pants away, uncaring where they landed.

"So many?"

"Call me an optimist." He gave her a cocky grin.

She dipped, pushing her breast into his hand as he rubbed obligingly over the distended nipple.

"Judging by the way you make me feel, I'd say you've got a good chance of being right."

"Now that's what I like to hear." He pinched her nipple, moving his other hand down from her hip to tangle in the curls at the apex of her thighs. He held her gaze as he slid one finger into her folds, finding the nub that craved his attention. He stroked her clit and her breath came in short gasps as her temperature rose.

She sat over his thighs, enjoying the wicked sensations for a moment before moving away. "No more of that for now. I want to come with you inside me, John." She almost blushed saying the words aloud, but the fire in his gaze told her he liked hearing her say such things.

She drew out the process of covering his cock with the condom, making sure John watched every step of the process. She wouldn't let him participate. When he tried to help, she pushed his hands away with a *tsk*ing sound. He gave in with good grace, letting her call the shots. She liked that. And she loved having him at her mercy, so to speak.

Before she finally rolled the condom over him, she took him in her mouth, just briefly. She would've spent more time there but he seemed too eager to let her play very long. Besides that, she wanted him desperately. There was something about the danger they'd shared earlier that spurred her libido to new heights. She didn't want to waste time. She wanted him now. Urgently.

Once he was covered, she rose over him, positioned him, and pushed downward. Damn, that felt good. He filled her so completely, so wonderfully. It was sheer bliss when he was inside her fully.

"Oh, yeah." The words popped out of her mouth without thought, without intention.

"Yeah," he echoed, drawing out the word, his expression intense as their gazes met and held. She began to ride him, slowly at first, then picking up speed as her passion increased.

John helped her when her thighs began to quiver under the strain. His hands gripped her hips, the muscles in his arms rippling as he lifted and lowered her. Even though she was on top, at some point, he'd taken control of the pace.

"Just like that, baby," he urged her in the sexiest voice ever. His eyes were half-lidded, his body hot beneath her and inside her. She loved the way he made her feel. The way he looked at her. The way he rocked her world.

"John! I need—" She couldn't finish the thought as her teeth clenched. She didn't know what she needed. She only hoped John did. She strained toward completion that was just out of her reach.

Until he reached down with one hand, his fingers stroking between her legs, rubbing her clit with urgent motions. Yes. That's just what she needed.

Donna screamed as she went off like a rocket, coming hard over him. John joined her a moment later, his body lifting hers as his muscles went rigid beneath her. She felt his spasms through her own as they joined in an orgasm that left her utterly replete.

Sighing as she floated downward, she settled her head against his chest and drifted for a long, pleasurable moment. Eventually, she was vaguely aware of John disengaging from her body and rolling them to their sides. She watched wearily as he took care of things quickly, then returned to her, tucking her back against his heart as she drifted off for a nap.

CHAPTER 6

The sound of a car parking behind theirs on the gravel drive under the trees alerted them. John rolled out of bed and began to dress.

"Go take your shower. I'll deal with these guys." John buttoned his shirt as he went out to meet the cleanup team.

The shower was lovely and restorative. She took a few minutes longer than she usually did, knowing John was occupied with the cleanup team. When she came out of the bathroom, she took a moment to tidy the bedroom.

Dressing in a fresh T-shirt and jeans from her knapsack, she headed out into the main room to find John. She paused to look out the window to see two very unfishermenlike-looking fishermen working near the porch. They had brand-new boots and clothing that looked as if they'd only snipped the tags off five minutes before they'd gotten there. Not only that, the clothes were ill-fitting as if someone else had bought them without regard for sizes. Donna stifled a laugh as she went toward the kitchen area where John stood.

"Are those guys for real?"

"Yeah, I know. They're not real good at camouflage, are they?" John chuckled as he handed her a cup of coffee. "If anyone asks, they're friends of ours from the city, just down for a little visit."

"They look more like city slickers than we do and we're both from New York." She chuckled and took a small sip of her coffee.

"Buzz there—the taller one—is from Georgia, and Willie is from New Orleans. Seems like neither one has ever been fishing before. They're both dyed-in-the-wool science geeks."

"Hey, you better watch that, bud. I'm a geek too."

John wrapped his arms around her waist and pulled her against him. "There's not a geeky bone in your luscious little body, sweetheart. Engineer or not."

"Mmm. I like that." She slipped her hands up under his T-shirt to stroke his solid six-pack of abdominal muscles. She loved the way his hard body rippled under her touch. She'd never been with a man who was more physically fit than John. Or more handsome. He was the complete package as far as she was concerned. Smart too. They related well now that they knew each other better.

"And I like you, sweetheart. Way more than a little."

His almost-declaration made her stomach clench as he leaned in to place a row of kisses along her cheek and jaw, working his way toward her mouth. When he finally reached his destination, his tongue slipped into her mouth and sent her temperature soaring.

A knock on the doorframe and a loud clearing of someone's throat easily heard through the screen door broke them apart all too soon. It was the taller member of the cleanup team. The one John had said was called Buzz.

Donna felt the heat of a blush in her cheeks as she walked toward the door.

"Your pardon for interrupting, ma'am." The fake fisherman had his funny fishing hat in his hands as he smiled at her. She could definitely hear the southern drawl of Georgia in his words.

"Not at all." She tried to ignore her own discomfort at being caught smooching another team member. "You're Buzz, right?" She opened the screen door and held out her hand. "I'm Donna."

He shook her hand gently and smiled again. "Pleased to meet you, Miss Donna." Oh, yeah, this man definitely had the charm of the Old South in his blood. "I just came to tell you we're done with the pickup and decon of the area. It was a little awkward having to hide most of our protective gear but we managed."

That explained the bad fit of their clothes to her mind. She hadn't realized they were wearing multiple layers. Close up now, she could see a few of the layers under the tacky and ill-fitting fake-fisherman clothes.

"I'm curious. What do you do with the remains?"

"Send them back to the lab for study. The team leaders are still trying to figure out how to return those remains that we can identify back to their next of kin. Mighty big mess if you ask me."

"Yeah, I guess I can see that." Donna jumped only a little when John came up beside her and put his left arm around her waist in a clear statement. Obviously he didn't care who knew they were together. She liked that. It made her feel warm inside.

"Thanks for coming out so quickly, Buzz." John held out his right hand to Buzz for a friendly shake.

"Happy to help, John. Most of the tracks come from the direction of the estate as far as we can tell. We did our best not to disturb anything so you can track back a ways. Mighty quiet in this camp. No people about to mess up the tracks and the nearest cabins are a ways back from yours. It's a good setup for this kind of operation, I'm thinking."

"We lucked out for sure," John agreed. "Luckily the darts don't make much noise at all or we'd have had the entire neighborhood down here earlier today. There's no one in the nearest cabins. I asked the landlord to put us out on the edge away from everyone else."

"Good thinking."

They talked a few minutes more and then Buzz took his leave. He and Willie left in a cloud of gravel dust as they rolled down the road out of the fishing camp. They took the remains with them and left the scene pristine and decontaminated.

John left to take a look at the tracks while Donna tidied up the cabin a bit. She also fixed a snack for them both, which they shared when John came back in.

"The sandwiches are good," John commented as they shared their snack at the small kitchen table, "but I'd like to take you out to dinner tonight for a change of pace. What do you think?"

"You mean like a date?" She held her breath waiting for his answer.

He moved closer to her. "Exactly like a date." His tone grew more intimate. "There's nothing in the operation manual that says we have to eat every meal in the cabin. If Sykes asks, we'll tell him we went scouting the area. Murray told me when we checked in that there's a nice restaurant with a scenic overlook a few miles up the road. I'd like to take you there."

Tingles went down her spine. "Okay, but I don't have anything too dressy with me."

"You're gorgeous in whatever you wear, Donna, but don't worry. Murray said the place is casual, with a five-star view, and down-home Southern cooking."

"I've never had really authentic Southern food."

"Then you're in for a treat."

Oh, yeah. She knew she was. Just being with John—on a real date—would be a treat.

The restaurant was lovely, perched on the side of a cliff overlooking a vast stretch of the lake far below. It took some maneuvering to get to the place and the sloped drive and parking lot was paved only with gravel, but the view alone was worth every difficulty to get there. The food was good, wholesome, Southern cooking and Donna enjoyed trying new dishes she hadn't even heard of before.

"The view here is amazing." Donna sighed as she gazed

out the window. They'd been seated by the window only after John had slipped a twenty to the hostess. He'd done it so smoothly, Donna hadn't even realized what had happened until after the fact. It gave her a little thrill to know he'd gone out of his way to make this dinner special.

"I agree. The lake...and the company." He raised his glass in her direction with a sexy wink. Oh, yeah. Her limbs were tingling, her blood singing with his nearness as he watched her over the rim of his wineglass. "It is a little odd though." He placed his glass back on the table, giving her a lopsided grin.

"How so?"

"I've never been on a date on a mission before," he admitted.

She laughed with him. "I guess this is pretty strange for you. This is only my first mission—probably my last as well—so I'm no expert."

"Oh, I think you have a bright future ahead of you, if you decide to go into covert work."

"You've got to be kidding," she scoffed good-naturedly.

"No, you've got a bead on looking the part. You don't have to act innocent. You're the real deal. Believe it or not, that's a big help. The owner of the fishing camp only had to glance at you and he gave me whatever I wanted. He bought my crazy-in-love-newlywed story hook, line, and sinker."

Another little thrill went through her at hearing the L-word coming from his lips. But she didn't dare think he might feel as strongly about her as she did about him. She didn't know when it had happened, but being here with him, in this moment out of time, was like a dream she'd never known she'd wanted to come true. He was magic. His every word, his every smile went straight to her heart.

She was on the verge of saying something all too revealing when a showy brunette swished down the crowded aisle toward their table. She must've been sitting in the private room off to one side. They could see the doors from where they sat, but hadn't been able to see inside. Donna looked up at the woman and her breath caught.

It was Dr. Bemkey. Donna recognized her from the photos in her file. She was much more intimidating in person, of course. Her perfect coiffure, manicured fingernails, and expertly applied makeup created a larger-than-life sort of presence that was backed up by the poise in every step. Designer clothes hung off her perfectly proportioned frame, and her ears, fingers, wrists, and neck dripped with gold and diamonds. All in all, she made a hell of a picture.

"Close your mouth, darling. You'll catch flies." Dr. Elizabeth Bemkey stopped before their table and addressed Donna directly before turning her attention to John. "I've seen you down by my beach," she said without blinking. "Please be sure to stay on the public side, lovey. You could get hurt and I wouldn't want to lose any more pets."

Did she mean…? Donna shot a quick look at John, but he had all his attention focused on the woman standing so calmly at the side of their table.

"I'm really very put out with you for interfering with my playthings." She tapped John on the shoulder as if she were some belle at an old-fashioned ball. Her smile was brittle and her eyes didn't look altogether sane. Donna felt a chill creep down her spine. "You'd better watch yourselves or you might end up becoming one of my toys." Her gaze turned ice cold.

She turned and walked out of the restaurant without even waiting for a response. Donna turned to John only after Dr. Bemkey was gone.

"What the hell was that?"

John's lips thinned as he frowned. "That was trouble with a capital *T*."

"She knows who we are?"

"At the very least she knows what we are and what we've been doing. She may not know our names, but she knows what we're doing down here."

"I think she threatened us." Donna was shocked. "She seemed mad as a hatter too."

"Yeah." John sat back in his chair and twirled his

wineglass. "She's crazy like a fox. And she needs to be run to ground."

"What?" Donna was afraid she understood what he meant all too well, but she needed confirmation.

"She doesn't seem stable and she issued a death threat. She doesn't know we're immune. But if she's running around threatening people, she's even more dangerous than I'd anticipated. In this kind of state, she could be capable of anything. We need to take her down now. As soon as possible." His gaze was hard as he looked out over the lake without really seeing it. He seemed focused on something much different and much deadlier.

They'd been on dessert when Dr. Bemkey had come over, so there was nothing keeping them at the restaurant. They paid the check and left the restaurant in short order. John had a faraway look on his face as he no doubt made plans that didn't include Donna. Or, if they did include her, only in a peripheral way. Donna was worried. She didn't like the idea of him operating out there all alone.

Originally, they'd thought they would watch, wait, and gather intel, taking out zombies along the way until they were ready to strike at Dr. Bemkey's lair—with help from the main team. Now, it looked like John planned to move up the timetable and forgo the promised help from the rest of the combat-able operatives on the team. Donna didn't know for sure, but she thought she knew John well enough by now to know the way he thought.

He drove them back down the cliff toward the cabin on the lakeshore without speaking much. Most likely, he was already planning the call he'd make when they got back to the cabin.

"Yes, sir. She came right up to our table, bold as brass, and issued a death threat." John was on the phone with Matt Sykes, pacing from window to window in the main room of the cabin. They'd returned only moments before and John had immediately phoned in his report to the commander.

"No, sir. I don't know how she knew who we were. She claimed to have seen us on the beach. It's possible she observed Donna that first night when her so-called *pet* chased Donna from the lakeshore. I'm not sure how she could've seen me unless there are some really well-hidden cameras there that I couldn't spot."

Donna listened to John's end of the conversation but she could figure out what was going on easily enough. John looked tense, like a coiled spring waiting to strike. She'd seen him like this before, when they were under attack. This was his moment. His element. This was what he'd been born to do.

"Yes, sir. I'm going out there tonight to take another look around," he said into the phone. She didn't like the sound of that at all. "No, sir. I won't take action unless it seems feasible and secure." There was a pause. "I understand. Thank you, sir."

He disconnected the call and stowed his phone in his pocket. Then he turned to her. "He still can't spare anyone to help."

Donna's heart sank. "I heard you say you were going out to do reconnaissance?"

"Yeah. Just a sneak and peek. I won't go in unless I think it's safe enough to do so." He armed himself from the box of ammunition the cleanup crew had restocked before they left.

"What if there are more zombies?" She hated the note of fear in her voice.

"I think we took out the bulk of them last night. Chances are she doesn't have that many of the creatures roaming around out here or there'd be a lot more missing people. Even way out here, if large numbers of people had gone missing, someone would have noticed by now." He prepared as he spoke, strapping on his utility belt and other gear. "Near as I can figure, she made the first few and then they went out and made the others. That takes time. I think we put quite a dent into her supply of *playthings* last night." He emphasized the word the crazy doctor had used to describe those she had killed.

"I can't believe she called them that." Donna was still shocked and a little disgusted with the woman's attitude.

"She's bonkers, babe. Which is why she needs to be taken down. The sooner the better. If she'd shown any sign of being more rational, I'd feel better. As it is, people in this kind of state are too unpredictable. We need to stop her."

"I can see that, but it won't stop me from worrying about you."

John stopped in front of her. "Don't worry, sweetheart. This is what I do." He held out his arms and she walked into them, grateful for his reassurance.

She wanted to cling to him but knew she had to let him go. "Just be careful out there, John."

"It's only a little recon. Depending on what I find, I'll either go in and take her down or come back here. No harm, no foul."

Everything looked quiet to John's trained eyes. Not too quiet. Just a normal foggy, creepy night on the lake. The ambiance was right out of a classic horror movie, but it didn't bother John. A little fog never hurt anyone. It was what might be hiding in the fog that could be the real problem. But his sixth sense told him nothing at the moment. Nothing stirred in the fog that shouldn't be there. The place was clear.

He'd crossed onto the estate's grounds twenty minutes before and had circled the big place twice. Nothing appeared out of place. If his third circuit of the grounds turned up nothing again, he'd go in closer. If he could take down his mark tonight, he would. That woman had to be stopped. The sooner the better.

He moved closer. He could see in the windows. There was no activity on the first floor even though there were lights on in almost every room. Security lights, most likely, on timers. The first floor didn't look lived in. The only place he could discern traffic was near the stairs. Footprints marred the lush pile of the carpet there, but nowhere else.

There was a balcony running along the back of the house that faced the water. If he could get up there, he could get a good look inside the second story. John looked for a likely tree and found one that wasn't ideal, but would do for his purposes.

A few minutes later, John was peeking into the upstairs windows. Bingo.

The doctor was moving between what looked like her bedroom and a dressing room, changing from the elegant dress she'd worn to the restaurant into something more casual. She tossed the dress over a chair and finished buttoning an expensive white shirt over equally pricey khaki pants. Both had little men riding polo ponies embroidered discreetly on them. The woman had a lot of money and didn't mind throwing it around. Her house was testament to that.

He looked around. The sun was almost completely gone now and the fog on the water had thickened even more. There was a chill in the air, but John didn't let the sinister atmosphere disturb him. The fog would cover his activities.

He had the perfect opportunity. Dr. Bemkey was alone in the house as far as he could tell, with no zombies around to defend her. He was going in.

He turned back to the window, but the light had gone out. The doctor was gone. She'd headed downstairs. Rather than take the risk of making a racket by going through the upper floor and stalking the woman down the stairs, he retreated to the tree so he could approach from the ground.

John dropped to the ground and thought about the most likely entrance he'd scoped out before. There were a set of glass double doors in the center of the back side of the house. John had used a tree at the end of the balcony closest to the woods.

"John!"

Donna's shout froze him in his tracks. He whipped around to find her running toward him from the tree line. What in the world was she doing? John went to her, surprised to see she had her pistol in one hand. Immediately, he looked around. The fog had moved in closer to the house. It obliterated almost everything, but he could see…movement. In the fog. Shit. The zombies had snuck up on him after all. He pulled his weapon and met Donna in the swirling mist.

"I saw them come up from the water." She spoke in an urgent whisper.

"Honey, you were supposed to wait at the cabin." John took only a moment to roll his eyes at her so she'd know he was only kidding. "Not that I'm complaining." He kept his voice low as they edged back toward the trees.

"I was watching the sunset over the lake when I saw something strange. John, they're actually hiding *in* the lake!"

"Son of a bitch." He shook his head. "That's a new one."

"They don't need to breathe," she went on in a whisper. "They can stay in the water all day while the sun is out and only come out of the water at night."

"I don't think they've seen us." They'd reached the tree line safely. John tucked Donna next to him under the cover of some thick branches as he watched the proceedings.

A cluster of dripping zombies paraded past them toward the house. A light clicked on in the upstairs room and the French doors opened to reveal Dr. Bemkey standing like some Eva Perón–wannabe on the balcony, ready to address her people.

"See that old guy at the front of the pack?" John whispered in Donna's ear. So far neither the creatures nor their creator had detected them. He wanted to keep it that way.

Donna nodded. Her eyes were glued to the action on the back lawn of the estate, but she was attuned to John's every word.

"Judging by the file photos I've seen, I'd say that's Dr. Bemkey's ex-husband. File said he left her for his secretary. I'd say the blond bimbo in the bikini is probably her."

"The others all look like fishermen. Mr. Bemkey isn't too damaged, but the rest all have bad bite marks. Dr. Bemkey probably made her ex her first victim and he made the others."

"I believe you're right." John was counting heads, trying to assess troop strength.

"Look at that big one. He looks like the fishing guide that advertises on those billboards."

"Bubba's Bass Tours." John remembered seeing that billboard as they drove here. Sure enough, the big guy from the sign looked a lot like the zombie that stood head and shoulders above the rest. Tall as well as wide, this guy was imposing. The creatures stopped beneath the balcony, all looking up at the woman above them. "Here we go. Evita's about to address the peons."

Donna stifled a laugh but John could tell she was nervous. Her body trembled in the chilly mist as she pressed against his side. She wasn't snuggling too close, but she seemed to need the bodily contact. He could understand that. This was a situation unlike any he'd ever been in before.

"My creations." Dr. Bemkey's voice floated down to them from the balcony. "Our time has come. Men have come to destroy you, but I want you to destroy them instead."

"Oh, shit." John felt his stomach drop as he reflexively checked his ammo supply.

"Your mistress wants you to go to the fishing camp. I want you to kill. Kill them all!"

The zombies began to stomp their feet and make those inhuman sounds. A few began to chant the word "kill."

"This can't be good." Donna looked from the zombies to John and back again. They were getting riled up into a frenzy.

"I counted twenty-three of them. I think we can take them, if we're smart about it."

"That sounds like an awful lot, John. Are you sure?" Donna's eyes were wide and fearful as she looked up at him in the misty darkness.

"The fog can work to our advantage. You just can't let too many of them track you at once."

"Now, my lovelies," Dr. Bemkey shouted from her balcony, "go now! Kill them all! Make me an army."

"Our time just ran out." John dragged her close for a quick kiss. "No matter what happens, I want you to know...I love you, Donna. It's crazy and it's sudden, but I love you more than any woman I've ever known."

"John..." Her reaction was a mixture of shock and what looked like joy, but it was dark and misty. And they had bigger fish to fry at the moment. He shouldn't have said anything, but he couldn't help himself.

"Go, sweetheart." He turned her around and pointed her toward the cabin. "Get all the ammo we've got left and meet me on the porch. I'll be right behind you. I just want to divert some of these guys first."

"Why?" she asked even as she took a step away, toward the cabin.

"Divide and conquer. We've got to get them into smaller groups so we can pick them off and they don't overwhelm us. I'll start that now while you get the ammo. We're going to need every last dart."

"Be careful." She gave him a pained look even as she sprang away through the trees toward the cabin.

John watched her go for only a moment before she was swallowed up by the swirling mist. John turned back to find the zombies heading slowly toward the tree line. All but one. It looked like Evita had held one back from the class: her ex-husband.

"Go jump in the lake," she ordered him and John wasn't all that surprised when he turned around and walked right back into the lake. Fine. That left twenty-two creatures for him and Donna to deal with. They'd handle Mr. Bemkey later.

CHAPTER 7

John came in hot, creatures on his trail as he hit the porch running. Donna was waiting there for him, bless her heart, with every dart and weapon in their small arsenal. She handed him a fresh clip before she said a word and he slammed it into his empty dart rifle.

"I'll reload this empty for you." She grabbed the empty clip he'd just taken from the weapon. Her small fingers deftly reloaded the clip with its deadly cargo and handed it back to him.

"You've got the pistols?"

"Yeah." She turned to show him her hip where one of the pistols rested in its holster. She handed the other to him.

"You keep it." He tried to hand it back.

"You fire faster and more accurately than I do. You need it more," she argued. "I'm good with the one I have and I packed plenty of ammunition in my bag."

He saw she had a canvas bag slung across her chest. It was the one that had been loaded with their pistol rounds.

"Open the bag. Let me see how much you have in there."

She turned the other way and lifted the flap on the rectangular bag. It was half full. She'd divvied up the pistol ammo to his satisfaction. She had about three quarters of their supply and he had the rest.

"Good. I want you to start down by the lake. Beware of anything coming from the water. There shouldn't be any left in there except Mr. Bemkey, but you never know. Start at the shoreline and work your way inward. Don't let anything get past you. We need to keep the zombies away from the other cabins. The line we don't want them to cross is from the lake to our cabin. I'll watch the woods on this side, you take the area from the lake to about halfway to here. We'll meet in the middle and overlap."

"All right." She looked scared but willing to do her part. Damn, he loved her courage and spirit as much as he loved her.

"Drop tags as you go if you can, but don't let it slow you down. We can always go back later to drop the transmitters."

She nodded, handing him the last clip and watching him stow it in a pouch on his utility belt. They were armed as well as they could be. He looked at her, wanting to say something meaningful but he saw her eyes widen as she peered over his shoulder.

He spun.

Damn. The zombies had found them.

"Be careful. Head for the water. I've got these guys." He gave her a quick kiss and vaulted off the porch. He hit the ground running, already firing darts at the zombies coming toward him.

They spent the next few hours zigzagging through the woods between the cabin and the lake, shooting zombies left and right. Some went down easy, some were more canny. Most were wearing fishing gear of one kind or another and John surmised that most of the victims had been fishermen, attacked while out for a day of leisure.

John met up with Donna every fifteen minutes or so as their paths intersected in the woods. The bulk of the creatures had come through the woods farther away from the waterline, as he'd hoped. So far, they were doing well. None had gotten through their defensive line. John still worried for

Donna's safety when she was out of his sight, but there was no help for it. They had a job to do and, so far, Donna was holding up well.

He was so proud of her. She'd stolen his heart with her smile and her personality. Her courage under fire impressed the hell out of him and only made him love her more.

The girl in the bikini had no doubt once been beautiful. Her silicone-enhanced breasts were now a thing of the past. The bikini was lopsided with prominent chunks of her flesh missing. She'd been chomped on by the zombies and the result wasn't pretty. Not at all.

Donna watched her disintegrate with a feeling of compassion. The girl—even if she had been a home-wrecking bimbo in life—hadn't deserved to die that way. Nobody deserved to die like that.

As she fell into a pile of goo at Donna's feet, something silver glinted in the grass, catching her eye. She bent down to take a closer look, using a stick to push the tattered remains of the bikini aside.

"What's this?"

John crouched to look over her shoulder.

"A tracker. And it's not one of ours." Donna looked up to catch his expression. His lips had thinned into a grim line. "That had to have been implanted beneath the skin. I've seen something like it before."

She didn't ask where. As a CIA operative, John had lots of secrets she would never be privy to. She knew better than to pry. If he said it was a tracking device, it damned well was a tracking device.

"You think Dr. Bemkey implanted it?" Donna stood, dropping the stick next to the remains. It would have to be collected and burned along with the rest of the surrounding debris that might now be contaminated.

"That would be my guess. This girl was her ex's mistress. Bemkey's crazy enough to want to keep tabs on her."

"So Dr. Bemkey probably knows she's gone, right?"

"Right." He checked his ammo and she did the same. She was down to a measly six darts. They would have to be enough. "We'd better get over to the mansion. With this one, our count is twenty-one. If my numbers are right, we've got two more to hunt down, plus their creator."

"I don't have enough ammo for two more. I've only got six darts left." But she was game. She walked fast, beside John as they crossed through the trees heading for the mansion's backyard.

"I've got eight. We need to make every shot count." He slowed as they reached the tree line.

The fog had dissipated. They could clearly see the lakeshore, though a fine mist still swirled above the water's surface. Dr. Bemkey paced on the sand, screaming. Her tone alternated from glee to anger and back again in violent swings of emotion.

"You stupid bastard! Your bimbo is gone. Do you hear me? Gone! And good riddance. She ruined my life and I took away hers. And you can't do a damned thing about it, you bastard."

"Oh, no." Donna saw something come out of the trees. "She doesn't see him."

It was Bubba. The tall wide mountain of a man who had towered over all the other creatures. He was heading right for the doctor and he looked hungry.

John was already running down the long expanse of lawn toward the lake. The doctor was still ranting, shaking her fist at the water and screaming. John fired as he ran, plugging the giant zombie with three darts in quick succession. Donna followed behind, saving her darts until she had a better shot. She couldn't fire on the run and hit anything the way John could.

John was still ten yards away when Bubba grabbed the doctor in his meaty fists. The woman screamed even more shrilly as Bubba sank his bloodstained teeth into her shoulder.

"Damn." John slowed to a stop and fired two more shots into the behemoth zombie. That made five. It had only taken four darts to stop the other creatures, but Donna agreed with John's unspoken reasoning. This guy was huge. If weight and height had anything to do with dosage—and it usually did—he'd need more than the usual four darts to take him down.

"John!" Donna saw Mr. Bemkey rising from the lake. He just walked straight out of the water and headed for Bubba and his struggling ex-wife.

"I see him." John fired another shot into Bubba. "Use your darts on the husband, Donna. I'm concentrating on Bubba for the moment. Four shots, Donna. The ex is normal size and we might need more for the big guy, the doc, and any stragglers who might show up."

Donna went to work, taking her shots carefully, making every one count. She shot at the ex-husband as he bit into his ex-wife's flesh, infecting her with the deadly contagion she'd invented. She'd killed him with it. It was a sort of poetic justice that he was doing the same to her.

But John and Donna had wanted to take her alive. They hadn't planned to kill her. The likelihood that she would survive this was small. They had the doomsday shot that had saved one person to date, but it wasn't perfected. It likely wouldn't work on the doctor. Still, they'd try. As soon as the coast was clear.

Donna paused to fire her last shot, taking aim and firing. Her darts were spaced out evenly over the ex-husband's body. If all went well, he should be disintegrating any minute now. All she had to do was wait. And withstand the screeching from the doctor as the two zombies continued to munch on her flesh.

"This big guy isn't going quietly," John muttered. "How many darts do you have left? Two?"

"Yeah. Two. That's it."

"I've got two. So between us we have enough to take down one more. Let's hope there aren't any more zombies down in that lake who decide to come up for a stroll right now."

Donna was too keyed up to smile, but she appreciated his

attempt at humor. They'd been through hell that night and it was almost over. They'd taken out a lot of dangerous creatures that night. Now all they had to do was wait out these last two and deal with the doctor.

"Finally." Donna heard the satisfaction in John's voice as he watched the struggling threesome on the beach. The big man named Bubba slithered to the ground, disintegrating before their eyes. The ex-husband followed suit a moment later. The doctor hit the sand with a splat as John and Donna ran over to her.

She was bleeding from multiple bites. Her eyes fluttered open as Donna reached her side.

"Is he dead? Is the cheating bastard really gone?"

"Yes, Dr. Bemkey. He's gone." Donna tried to break the news gently.

A cackling laugh was the doctor's response. Her eyes flared wildly, showing the whites around her dilated pupils and shocky irises. "Good riddance to bad rubbish, I say. My only regret is that the bastard managed to take me with him."

"Maybe not." John had been working steadily, removing things from his utility belt as he prepared the Hail Mary dose that just might save the woman's life if she was one of the lucky ones.

"Don't be silly, boy. The contagion kills. It kills everyone."

"It didn't kill me," Donna said softly, dragging the woman's attention back to her. "I was attacked and I didn't die. I'm naturally immune."

"No such thing." The doctor looked scandalized and very upset that her killing cocktail wasn't one-hundred-percent efficient.

"I'm afraid you're wrong."

"And this could save you, Doctor. Brace yourself." John aimed the long needle for the doctor's heart. He paused only a moment to perfect his aim, then pushed it inward and depressed the plunger. The doctor screamed as the needle went into her flesh.

"You stupid son of a bitch!" Dr. Bemkey raged. "That

hurt."

"It might save you, it might not." John removed the needle and sat back on his haunches. "Frankly, the chances are slim, but we had to try. Do you have any final messages? Maybe to your business partners? Now's your time to come clean. You may never get another chance to drag them down with you."

"Why would I want to do that?" The doctor seemed to lose strength before their eyes. "Juan is my lover as well as my business partner. I wouldn't hurt him for the world."

"Juan? Juan who?" John prodded.

"Nice try." Dr. Bemkey turned her head as she began to fade. "Juan's identity will go with me to my grave. But I'll give you one tidbit before I go. Zalayat. Berthold Zalayat. The evil bastard cheated me and called me crazy. Take him down and I'll have my revenge."

"Where do we find him?" John pushed, but the woman was gone. Her eyes closed and her breathing stopped. She was dead. "Damn." John put away the special serum and took a deep breath before moving on. "We'll take her inside and keep an eye on her. If she rises, we'll use the last of our darts. This has been one hell of a night."

The gray light of dawn gave way to the pink and gold of true sunlight as they sat there, looking at each other. Donna greeted the sun with enthusiasm. If the sun was out, the zombies—if any still existed—would be in hiding.

John stood and lifted the doctor's body into his arms. He strode to the mansion at a fast clip and Donna did her best to keep up. She preceded him to the double glass doors and found them open. Dr. Bemkey must have come out this way and left the door open behind her. Convenient. Donna threw the doors open wide ahead of John and his gruesome burden.

She went ahead of him into the house. He placed Dr. Bemkey down on a chaise longue near the back door. He then stalked through the lower floor of the two-story mansion, checking each room while she followed.

"The place looks okay. I'll watch over her and call the

cavalry. We have to go out there and drop markers for the cleanup team."

"I'll do the two at the beach. I marked all my other targets along the way."

"Good girl. So did I. So it's just those last two, and her...." he looked over at the body by the door. "Run down to the beach and mark them. I'll watch you from here while I make the call. We can't leave her unattended."

Donna ran outside and dropped the markers quickly, walking back to the house at a slower pace, enjoying a quiet moment in the early morning sun. By the time she got back to the mansion, John had hung up the phone.

"We're staying here for the day. I called the cleanup team. They'll be here in about an hour. I also reported to the commander. He wants us to search this place, but we need sleep too. I saw a guest room down the hall, or you can sack out on the couch until the cleanup guys get here."

Donna didn't want to leave him in the lurch, but now that the excitement was over, the adrenaline rush that had kept her going was leaving her drained. "I'll lie down on the couch for a few minutes. I'm not used to these all-nighters anymore." She smiled at him, weariness sapping her energy. "But if you need me, just let me know. I don't want to leave you shorthanded."

John caught her hand as she passed him on her way to the couch. He reeled her in and placed a lingering kiss on her lips.

"You're perfect, Donna." He smiled at her as he let her go. "Get some rest while you can. We're going to have a busy day."

He wasn't kidding. Donna napped for only about forty-five minutes before the cleanup crew arrived in the house. They took Dr. Bemkey's body away. She hadn't risen...yet. But they had the equipment to deal with her if and when she did. They also replenished John's supply of toxic darts. He split the wealth with Donna when he saw that she'd awakened.

"The guys will be working out there for the next few

hours," John told her, sitting on the edge of the couch. He stroked her cheek with the fingers of one hand. "There's a nice guest room at the end of the hall. Why don't you go in there and get some real rest? I'll join you in a bit. We can sleep while Buzz keeps an eye out. We're both wiped out after last night."

"Are you sure?" It sounded heavenly, but could they really afford the time away from the mission?

"Yeah." He stood and ushered her to her feet. "Let's get you to bed."

"Oh, I like the sound of that." She couldn't resist teasing him as they walked down the sumptuously carpeted hallway.

"Vixen." His voice growled in her ear as he bent to nibble playfully on her earlobe. "Sleep first. Then work. Then fun and games. If you're good."

CHAPTER 8

Donna woke to warmth. John knelt over her, his big body cocooning her in his heat, his masculine strength. She loved the sensation. As much as she loved him.

He'd told her he loved her, if that speedy declaration could be believed. She'd have to hear it again to be sure. She knew people said things sometimes in extreme circumstances that wouldn't necessarily hold true later. She prayed that wasn't the case here. She loved John with all her heart and wanted his love in return. It would be a dream come true if he really had meant what he'd said.

"Stop faking. I know you're awake." His voice growled near her ear before he placed a sharp nip on her earlobe that made her yelp and laugh at the same time.

"How can you be so sure?" She kept her eyes closed, rubbing her cheek against his.

"I'm a highly trained CIA operative. It's my business to know these kinds of things." His mouth drifted down over hers as he crawled over her on the bed, bracketing her with his knees on either side of her thighs and his forearms beside her head.

Their kiss was filled with languorous wonder. It was a slow exploration of a kind they had never shared before. There had always been a hurried quality to their encounters—even the slow times. There was always a sense that they were on the job and couldn't spend too much time away from the mission.

That was gone now. John's kiss drugged her, dragging her under with him where he was her anchor, her safety line, and the very air she breathed. She trusted his passion to guide her own.

"I thought we were going to save the fun and games for later." She smiled playfully at him when he let her up for air.

"I decided it couldn't wait. Buzz is keeping watch outside while we rest. We'll sleep…eventually." His wicked grin rocked her world. "But loving you couldn't wait."

Her breath caught at his words and the look in his beautiful eyes. He paused.

"What? You didn't believe me before?" His smile cajoled but there were serious depths to his words. "I love you, Donna."

She was stunned by the sincerity in his expression, the way he put himself out there on the ledge. She'd never had a man be so open with her. Never.

"Hey, babe, tell me I'm not alone here." Doubt crept over his features and she rushed to reassure him.

"You're not alone." She felt her cheeks flush with excitement. "I love you too, John. I just thought—"

"What? What did you think?" He moved closer again, nuzzling the tip of her nose with his.

"I thought maybe, now that things have calmed down…"

"That I'd take back what I told you in the woods?" He pulled back, a chastising look on his face. "Oh, baby. You'll learn I never say anything I don't mean. And I've never said the L-word to any woman before."

"That sounds serious." She was basking in the moment. He had the most delicious way of speaking and the way he looked at her melted her heart.

"Very serious." He moved in for a quick kiss that ended too soon. "Like, rest of our lives serious." He kissed her again and drew back with obvious reluctance. "Damn, I was going to wait for the right time, but I can't wait. Donna, I know I'm no prize, but I can't see living without you. I need you in my life, uncertain as it is. I figure you've already seen me at my worst and you know what I do for a living. There are no secrets between us and I've never had that with anyone before. You see me as I am and yet you still seem to like me." He chuckled at his own words as tears filled her eyes. "Will you marry me?"

"Yes!" She could only manage the single word as emotion overtook her. It didn't matter though, as his lips covered hers, his body sheltering her in his warmth.

Their clothes disappeared as their temperature rose. The loving was slow and sensuous, with none of the urgency that had marked their previous times together. They were in tune physically, mentally, and emotionally. She felt it in his kiss and in his touch.

John licked his way down her body and back up, pausing at all the interesting points in between. He paid special attention to her breasts, drawing on her nipples with wet, warm suction that made her arch off the bed in pleasure.

She wanted to touch him but he wouldn't let her. He took both her wrists and placed them against the headboard with an admonishing look.

"Keep them there, Donna. I mean it."

"Or what?" she dared to challenge him.

"Bad girls get punished, baby." He winked at her.

"Sounds like it might be fun to be bad."

He pretended to consider. "It could be at that, but let's save that for another time. This is special. It's the first time I'm making love to my fiancée."

"Fiancée." She marveled at the word. "I really love the sound of that."

"Mmm." He nuzzled her neck. "Me too. As much as I love you." He looked deeply into her eyes. "I love the way you stand up to me and with me. I never expected to feel this way about anyone, Donna."

Her stomach clenched at the honesty in his eyes.

"I never expected this, John, but I hoped. Even when I shouldn't have, I hoped you'd want me. I've never met anyone like you before. From the beginning, we've fit together."

His gaze turned wicked. "Oh, yeah. We fit together perfectly." He nipped her earlobe. "Let me remind you."

Her excitement was already spiking with need. Having John naked in her bed and against her body did that to her. He turned her on like no man before. She lay under him, willing to do whatever he wanted, wanting to bask in this first time—as he'd called it—being with the man she loved, knowing he loved her in return.

Just knowing they'd admitted such intimate feelings made the whole experience all that much more special. She felt alive in a way she had only ever experienced with John as he brought her senses to a peak with hot strokes of his tongue over her most sensitive places.

When he joined his body to hers, she moaned with pleasure, welcoming him.

"You feel so good, Donna," he gasped near her ear as he lowered his body over hers, blanketing her in his warmth and strength.

"So do you." Her voice was breathless as her fever rose. Then he began to move and she lost the ability to speak at all.

Long, slow strokes interspersed with hard jolts made her sigh in delight. He kept her guessing and kept her arousal on the knife's edge between passion and ecstasy. She felt his body gathering for the coming explosion and joined him, riding the tide of pleasure along with him.

When the wave broke over them, it swept them up in unison, awash in bliss. He held her through the tremors of her completion, giving and taking with equal measure as they shared the most perfect moment ever.

A long time later, they let each other go by slow degrees. John looked into her eyes, a wide grin on his face and love in his gaze. She basked in that look, knowing it was just for her.

And she let her own feelings show as she gazed back.

"I love you so much, John." She lifted her hand to stroke his cheek. He turned his head and dropped a kiss in her palm.

He rolled away and tucked her close, spooning with her from behind.

"Let's get some sleep. Buzz will wake us before the cleanup team leaves."

She drifted off as John settled the soft comforter around them, too tired and sated to stay awake any longer.

In the late afternoon, John left the bed. He let Donna sleep while he did a thorough search of the mansion. The cleanup guys were still hard at work. He'd wake Donna up before they left, but he didn't have the heart to rouse her yet. She was tuckered out from the night they'd spent in the woods chasing zombies. Hopefully, there wouldn't be too many more nights like that in their future.

The fact that they had a shared future still amazed him. He'd never felt such love in his heart for a woman, never admired one or cared for one so deeply. That she felt the same about him in return still made him grin like a fool. There was no doubt they'd signed on for a tough mission chasing zombies and bad guys who wanted to zombify the world, but they'd face whatever came together.

He'd never had that before. Sure, he'd worked with team members and comrades in arms that were like brothers, but he'd never been part of a couple like this before. He worried about her working in the field, but he'd worry more if he weren't able to be there with her, watching her back. She'd already proven she could handle herself well. With his tutelage, she'd have every advantage to come out alive from the situations in which they'd no doubt find themselves in the future.

She taught him things too. She'd sharpened his appreciation for scientific method and protocols. She was one of the most intelligent and quick-witted women he'd ever been with and he was still a little amazed that she'd fallen in love with him. He wasn't questioning it. He wouldn't point out that he was probably getting away with something. If she was willing to be his, he'd take her on any terms. He loved her that much.

His only worry was how the rest of the team would react to their return to base as a couple. Would she want to hide their relationship? Would she be embarrassed by him? He wasn't sure and it was driving him a little crazy.

They'd talked about their feelings, but they hadn't talked about how those feelings and this new relationship would work day to day, working together with the rest of the team. Maybe he was borrowing trouble but Donna was such a special woman, he didn't want to hide his love for her. He was prepared to take the teasing—maybe even a reprimand or two from some of the more stodgy higher-ups—but was she?

He didn't want their relationship to make her uncomfortable. He knew how some of the guys would react with teasing and even lewd remarks. He'd clobber anyone who said anything disrespectful around Donna, but the possibility was there. He didn't know the rest of the team that well yet. They seemed like good guys but he wasn't one hundred percent sure of them all yet. Time would tell.

He only hoped Donna was willing to give him the time. In the back of his mind he still worried that she'd jumped headlong into this relationship too fast. He worried that circumstances had thrown them together and somehow she'd wake up and realize she'd made a mistake in thinking she loved him.

He planned to tie her to him and convince her that was where she really wanted to be before anything like that could happen. She was the best thing that had ever happened to him and he wasn't about to let her go.

John was thinking about all this as he searched the big house from top to bottom. Nearing the end of his search, he finally found what he was looking for. A secret room was built cleverly into the house, hidden in the architecture so well, he'd almost missed it.

Inside, he found the doctor's secret lab, along with all her notes and files, a computer, and a laptop.

"John?" Donna's voice came to him faintly from another part of the house.

"I'm in the west wing," he shouted back.

Before long, he heard her footsteps drawing closer.

"In here, Donna."

A few more footsteps drew closer and then her head peeked into the hidden room.

"What is this place and how in the world did you find it?"

"It's a hidden laboratory. Every self-respecting mad scientist has one. Didn't you know?" He grinned at her as she advanced into the room.

"What did you find?"

"Paydirt. There's a complete list of all the rogue science team members and their foreign contacts. Dr. Bemkey may have been insane toward the end, but she was meticulous. Her lab is spotless and all her notes on the experiments she was conducting are neat and tidy. I already forwarded all the electronic files to the team at Fort Bragg. We can leave the paper documents for the techs to decontaminate and package up for shipment as soon as they've dealt with the zombie remains."

"Wow. This is really good." She paged through one of the notebooks on the table. "I bet the docs back at base will learn a lot from this."

"No doubt," John agreed, moving close to her and swooping in for a quick kiss. "Damn, I needed that."

"Mmm. Me too." Her fingers stroked over his chest in a way that made him want to forget all about the work they had yet to do.

He cuddled her for a while but he knew he had to get back on track with the mission so they could wrap things up and head home to base. What kind of reception they'd get once the commander realized they'd become a couple, John wasn't sure. There wasn't really a chain-of-command issue. They both worked on the same team but for different branches.

Donna wasn't CIA, so fraternizing wouldn't really be an issue unless Commander Sykes wanted to make it into one. Judging by the way he'd seemed to accept Sarah and Xavier's engagement, John didn't expect too much trouble from that direction.

The possible complications could come from higher up or from the other team members. The other guys would tease the hell out of John for hooking up with his first female partner. First, last, and only, as far as John was concerned. Donna was it for him. The other guys would just have to deal with it.

"The cleanup team is finishing up," Donna said, her head tucked under his chin. "They brought some stuff we could make for dinner if you're interested."

At the mention of food, his stomach rumbled. She laughed.

"I guess we should eat. Once it gets dark, we'll have to do some patrolling to make sure we got them all last night."

"I hope we don't find any more of them." She shuddered and pulled away. He let her go but followed her out the door of the hidden room.

"I honestly don't think we will." John took her hand as they went through the house, just wanting to touch her. "But we need to be absolutely certain before we call this done."

They ended up in the kitchen where a few MREs were waiting for them on the center island, courtesy of the cleanup team. Donna dug into the packages with gusto, reading the directions. John was well familiar with the Meals Ready to Eat and didn't have to waste time figuring out which packets held what and how to prepare them. He tore in and started handing stuff to her that he thought she'd like.

They played with their food like kids, throwing morsels into each other's mouths and clowning around with lots of laughter and love. John had never had so much fun with a couple of MREs. It was Donna that made all the difference.

"Do we really have to go out there?" Donna's gaze was caught by the setting sun out the window.

"You don't." John covered her hand on the table, drawing her attention. "But I'm going out to do the check. You can stay in here. It's safe. The creatures weren't able to get in here while the doc lived here."

"Yet they still got her." Donna shivered at the memory and John took her hand in both of his, drawing closer.

"Only because she went outside to nag her husband. Let that be a lesson for the future."

She burst out laughing as he'd hoped she would and the disturbing memory left her eyes.

"I'd never nag you, John. Maybe just…forcefully remind you of things now and again."

He pulled her in for a quick hug. "I think I can live with that."

John patrolled the woods around the house and the fishing camp most of the night. Thankfully, all was quiet. Donna had volunteered to come out with him, despite her obvious reluctance. She was a trooper. He admired the hell out of her courage and willingness to do the hard jobs.

He'd left her inside, cataloging some of the scientific evidence they'd found in the hidden room. The last time he'd cruised into the mansion to check on her, she'd been on the phone with some of the other team members, relaying newly discovered information.

He'd checked in with the team leader earlier and received new orders. If he found no evidence of further zombie activity in the area tonight, they were to hightail it back to North Carolina. The team there was still in trouble and needed help. John was more than willing to enter the fight back on base, now that he could fully join the combat team. It had been hard for him to sit on the sidelines in a support role. He'd done it in order to be involved in the mission in which his little sister was so heavily involved. Meeting Donna had been a fortunate twist of fate.

Who knew he'd find his soul mate on a top-secret mission? John still couldn't quite believe it. For sure his sister,

Sarah, was going to be surprised. John smiled as he thought of his little sister. The smile widened as he finished his last circuit before dawn with nary a sign of a zombie. The place was clear. They'd gotten all the creatures the night before, thank goodness.

Donna was waiting for him with open arms. He stepped into her embrace and swept her into a hug that made her squeal as he swung her around. He dipped his head and gave her a smacking kiss.

"Now that's something to come home to." He loved the way she smiled at him with that soft look in her eyes just for him.

"But we're not *home*." She rolled her eyes around at the mansion that was serving as their base for the moment.

"Anywhere you are is home to me, Donna."

"That is the sweetest thing anyone's ever said to me."

She actually teared up. Damn. He hadn't meant to make her cry. John dipped his head and kissed away the tears as gently as he could, which only seemed to make it worse. Double damn.

"Don't mind me." She tried to downplay her emotional response and he let her.

"You're beautiful, Donna." He set her a little away from him. He couldn't let her go completely, but he walked by her side as they entered the mansion. "So what have you been up to while I was out chasing shadows?"

"I found a lot of great information and sent it back to the docs at the base. I was on the phone with them most of the night, in fact."

"Do you think you got it all? Or is there more to discover here?"

"There's probably a lot more good information to discover, but it's beyond my technical skill. I think I hit the most important stuff for now, but the lab contents have got to be boxed up and sent back to the science team."

"Good. Buzz is going to do that while we head back to Fort Bragg tomorrow." He paused as she turned to face him inside the giant kitchen of the posh house.

"You got new orders?"

He nodded. "We both did. I spoke to Commander Sykes a couple of hours ago. They've still got big problems on base and need all hands on deck. We're heading back to North Carolina. You okay with that?"

"Yeah, I guess. So you didn't find anything in the woods?"

"Not a trace. I think it's safe to say that we got them all." He hooked his thumbs into his utility belt as he leaned back against the kitchen counter.

"Thank goodness."

"We have to drive to Knoxville this morning and we'll catch a flight from there. You ready to face the rest of the team as a couple?" He laid his worries on the line. He wouldn't hide their new relationship. He wanted her to acknowledge his claim to all and sundry.

"Sure, why not?"

Her easy acceptance floored him. In a flash, he realized he'd made a mountain out of a molehill. She'd never know how uneasy he'd been. No, that would remain his little secret.

"Yeah, why not?"

He laughed at himself and hugged her close. Damn, his woman was perfect.

They packed up and headed for Knoxville a couple of hours later and were back at Fort Bragg that night. John was proud of his new fiancée when they reported to Commander Sykes's office for a full debrief. She took the bull by the horns, so to speak, surprising both men.

"Commander," she spoke forcefully as he motioned for them to take the chairs in front of his desk, "John and I are engaged. Is that a problem?"

Sykes sat back in his chair and just looked at them for a long minute while John's tension mounted. Then a slow grin stole over the commander's face.

"I can't say that I ever intended to run a team quite like this before. Seems like Noah's Ark around here lately with everyone pairing off, two by two. But I have no objection. In fact, I'm very happy for you. Congratulations to you both." Sykes leaned forward to shake both their hands, his smile genuine and friendly.

"Thank you, sir," John replied, a little stymied by the man's easy acceptance.

As usual, Donna was more open with her reaction. She gave Sykes a quick hug and accepted a friendly kiss on her cheek.

"Thanks, Matt. And thanks for pairing us up to begin with. I guess, in a way, we owe our happiness to you."

Sykes held up his hands, palms outward. "Oh, I can't take credit for this. This is all on you two. And if the brass gets on my case, you can be sure that's exactly what I'll tell them."

They all laughed. John knew in his heart that Matt Sykes wouldn't hang them out to dry. No, the commander was definitely on their side and he'd go to bat for them if necessary. He was that kind of guy.

John didn't know how he'd gotten so lucky. Sure, being picked for a team that had to fight zombies in total secrecy wasn't really the greatest stroke of luck, but it turned out to be a blessing in disguise. Not only had he found a mission that got his blood pumping, but he'd found a woman who would complete his world now and for as long as they were blessed to be together. If he had anything to say about it, he'd keep her forever.

Donna turned to him and took his hand. It was an inappropriate move in a military office, but he said nothing. When she looked at him with those beautiful eyes full of love, he'd give her anything. His heart, his soul, his life. And most especially, his love.

EPILOGUE

Somewhere in North Carolina

"Bemkey, the crazy bitch, offed Wallace. He was our main contact at Praxis Air."

"I told you she was going to be trouble," the man complained.

"It couldn't be helped. She was part of the original team. She knew too much. She had to be let in. I never planned to leave her around for long, though. She was a good scientist, but personally she was a liability."

"Was?" The man sounded curious.

"She's dead. One of the zombies must've got her or there would've been more to bury. I got the news through our source in the mailroom a half hour ago."

"Can't say I'm sorry. In fact, I'm glad we don't have to worry about her anymore. She was a loose cannon."

"I agree. But we'll have to cultivate our other contact at the airline. We need them."

"Not to worry. I've got some leverage against one of the owners. Praxis Air won't be a problem."

"You're sure?"
"Positive. Leave it to me."

#

ABOUT THE AUTHOR

Bianca D'Arc has run a laboratory, climbed the corporate ladder in the shark-infested streets of lower Manhattan, studied and taught martial arts, and earned the right to put a whole bunch of letters after her name, but she's always enjoyed writing more than any of her other pursuits. She grew up and still lives on Long Island, where she keeps busy with an extensive garden, several aquariums full of very demanding fish, and writing her favorite genres of paranormal, fantasy and sci-fi romance.

Bianca loves to hear from readers and can be reached through Twitter (@BiancaDArc), Facebook (BiancaDArcAuthor) or through the various links on her website.

WELCOME TO THE D'ARC SIDE…
WWW.BIANCADARC.COM

OTHER BOOKS BY BIANCA D'ARC

Brotherhood of Blood
One & Only
Rare Vintage
Phantom Desires
Sweeter Than Wine
Forever Valentine
Wolf Hills*
Wolf Quest

Tales of the Were
Lords of the Were
Inferno

Tales of the Were ~
The Others
Rocky
Slade

Tales of the Were ~
String of Fate
Cat's Cradle
King's Throne
Jacob's Ladder
Her Warriors

Tales of the Were ~
Redstone Clan
The Purrfect Stranger
Grif
Red
Magnus
Bobcat
Matt

Tales of the Were ~
Grizzly Cove
All About the Bear
Mating Dance
Night Shift
Alpha Bear
Saving Grace
Bearliest Catch
The Bear's Healing Touch
The Luck of the Shifters
Badass Bear

Tales of the Were ~
Were-Fey Love Story
Lone Wolf
Snow Magic
Midnight Kiss

Tales of the Were ~
Jaguar Island (Howls)
The Jaguar Tycoon
The Jaguar Bodyguard

Gemini Project
Tag Team
Doubling Down

Resonance Mates
Hara's Legacy**
Davin's Quest
Jaci's Experiment
Grady's Awakening
Harry's Sacrifice

Dragon Knights

Daughters of the Dragon
Maiden Flight*
Border Lair
The Ice Dragon**
Prince of Spies***

Dragon Knights ~ Novellas
The Dragon Healer
Master at Arms
Wings of Change

Sons of Draconia
FireDrake
Dragon Storm
Keeper of the Flame
Hidden Dragons

The Sea Captain's Daughter
Book 1: Sea Dragon
Book 2: Dragon Fire
Book 3: Dragon Mates

Guardians of the Dark
Half Past Dead
Once Bitten, Twice Dead
A Darker Shade of Dead
The Beast Within
Dead Alert

StarLords
Hidden Talent
Talent For Trouble
Shy Talent

Jit'Suku Chronicles ~ Arcana
King of Swords
King of Cups
King of Clubs
King of Stars
End of the Line
Diva

Jit'Suku Chronicles ~ Sons of Amber
Angel in the Badlands
Master of Her Heart

StarLords
Hidden Talent
Talent For Trouble
Shy Talent

Gifts of the Ancients
Warrior's Heart

* RT Book Reviews Awards Nominee
** EPPIE Award Winner
*** CAPA Award Winner

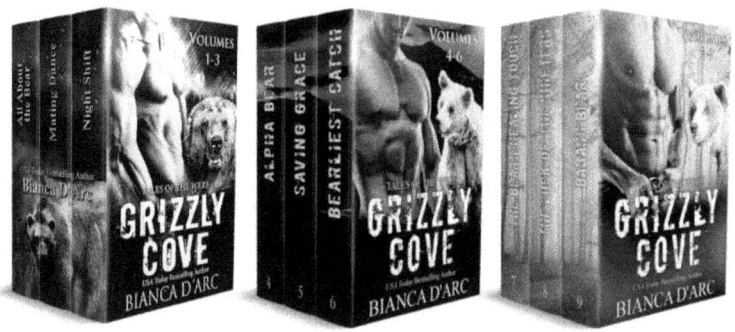

Welcome to Grizzly Cove, where bear shifters can be who they are - if the creatures of the deep will just leave them be. Wild magic, unexpected allies, a conflagration of sorcery and shifter magic the likes of which has not been seen in centuries... That's what awaits the peaceful town of Grizzly Cove. That, and love. Lots and lots of love.

This series begins with...

All About the Bear
Welcome to Grizzly Cove, where the sheriff has more than the peace to protect. The proprietor of the new bakery in town is clueless about the dual nature of her nearest neighbors, but not for long. It'll be up to Sheriff Brody to clue her in and convince her to stay calm—and in his bed—for the next fifty years or so.

Mating Dance
Tom, Grizzly Cove's only lawyer, is also a badass grizzly bear, but he's met his match in Ashley, the woman he just can't get out of his mind. She's got a dark secret, that only he knows. When ugliness from her past tracks her to her new home, can Tom protect the woman he is fast coming to believe is his mate?

Night Shift
Sheriff's Deputy Zak is one of the few black bear shifters in a colony of grizzlies. When his job takes him into closer proximity to the lovely Tina, though, he finds he can't resist her. Could it be he's finally found his mate? And when adversity strikes, will she turn to him, or run into the night? Zak will do all he can to make sure she chooses him.

Phoenix Rising

Lance is inexplicably drawn to the sun and doesn't understand why. Tina is a witch who remembers him from their high school days. She'd had a crush on the quiet boy who had an air of magic about him. Reunited by Fate, she wonders if she could be the one to ground him and make him want to stay even after the fire within him claims his soul...if only their love can be strong enough.

Phoenix and the Wolf

Diana is drawn to the sun and dreams of flying, but her elderly grandmother needs her feet firmly on the ground. When Diana's old clunker breaks down in front of a high-end car lot, she seeks help and finds herself ensnared by the sexy werewolf mechanic who runs the repair shop. Stone makes her want to forget all her responsibilities and take a walk on the wild side...with him.

Phoenix and the Dragon

He's a dragon shapeshifter in search of others like himself. She's a newly transformed phoenix shifter with a lot to learn and bad guys on her trail. Together, they will go on a dazzling adventure into the unknown, and fight against evil folk intent on subduing her immense power and using it for their own ends. They will face untold danger and find love that will last a lifetime.

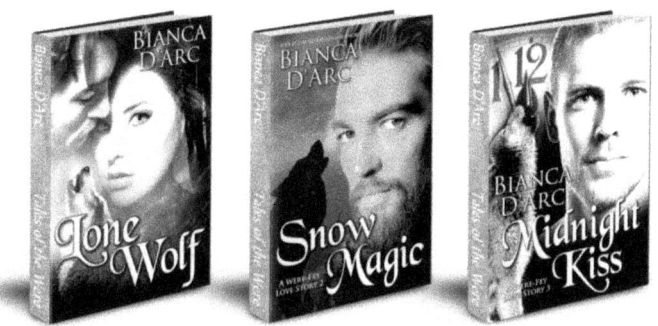

Lone Wolf

Josh is a werewolf who suddenly has extra, unexpected and totally untrained powers. He's not happy about it - or about the evil jackasses who keep attacking him, trying to steal his magic. Forced to seek help, Josh is sent to an unexpected ally for training.

Deena is a priestess with more than her share of magical power and a unique ability that has made her a target. She welcomes Josh, seeing a kindred soul in the lone werewolf. She knows she can help him... if they can survive their enemies long enough.

Snow Magic

Evie has been a lone wolf since the disappearance of her mate, Sir Rayburne, a fey knight from another realm. Left all alone with a young son to raise, Evie has become stronger than she ever was. But now her son is grown and suddenly Ray is back.

Ray never meant to leave Evie all those years ago but he's been caught in a magical trap, slowly being drained of magic all this time. Freed at last, he whisks Evie to the only place he knows in the mortal realm where they were happy and safe—the rustic cabin in the midst of a North Dakota winter where they had been newlyweds. He's used the last of his magic to get there and until he recovers a bit, they're stuck in the middle of nowhere with a blizzard coming and bad guys on their trail.

Can they pick up where they left off and rekindle the magic between them, or has it been extinguished forever?

Midnight Kiss

Margo is a werewolf on a mission...with a disruptively handsome mage named Gabe. She can't figure out where Gabe fits in the pecking order, but it doesn't seem to matter to the attraction driving her wild. Gabe knows he's going to have to prove himself in order to win Margo's heart. He wants her for his mate, but can she give her heart to a mage? And will their dangerous quest get in the way?

The Jaguar Tycoon
Mark may be the larger-than-life billionaire Alpha of the secretive Jaguar Clan, but he's a pussycat when it comes to the one women destined to be his mate. Shelly is an up-and-coming architect trying to drum up business at an elite dinner party at which Mark is the guest of honor. When shots ring out, the hunt for the gunman brings Mark into Shelly's path and their lives will never be the same.

The Jaguar Bodyguard
Sworn to protect his Clan, Nick heads to Hollywood to keep an eye on a rising star who has seen a little too much for her own good. Unexpectedly fame has made a circus of Sal's life, but when decapitated squirrels show up on her doorstep, she knows she needs professional help. Nick embeds himself in her security squad to keep an eye on her as sparks fly and passions rise between them. Can he keep her safe and prevent her from revealing what she knows?

The Jaguar's Secret Baby
Hank has never forgotten the wild woman with whom he spent one memorable night. He's dreamed of her for years now, but has never been back to the small airport in Texas owned and run by her werewolf Pack. Tracy was left with a delicious memory of her night in Hank's arms, and a beautiful baby girl who is the light of her life. She chose not to tell Hank about his daughter, but when he finally returns and he discovers the daughter he's never known, he'll do all he can to set things right.

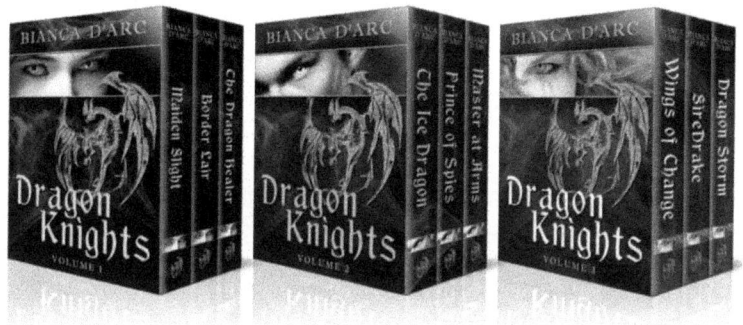

Dragon Knights

Two dragons, two knights, and one woman to complete their circle. That's the recipe for happiness in the land of fighting dragons. But there are a few special dragons that are more. They are the ruling family and they are half-dragon and half-human, able to change at will from one form to another.

Books in this series have won the EPPIE Award for Best Erotic Romance in the Fantasy/Paranormal category, and have been nominated for RT Reviewers Choice Awards among other honors.

The first three novellas in the critically acclaimed vampire romance series...

One & Only
Atticus is about to give up and greet the sun when he finds the love of his eternal life...by accident.

Rare Vintage
Marc, Master vampire of the Napa Valley, can't keep away from Kelly, no matter how many sparks fly between them. When an enemy challenges his authority, will she sacrifice her life for his?

Phantom Desires
Master Dmitri's lair is located under a farmhouse in rural Wyoming. Spying on the new owner while she sleeps could be more dangerous than even he suspects.

Rocky

Maggie is on the run from a killer, directly into the arms of Rocky, a man from her past. He's much more than a man, though. He's a shapeshifter. A grizzly bear who can protect her and her babies from the demon who murdered their father - Rocky's childhood friend. Magic, fists, claws and blood will determine the winner when the demon tracks Maggie to his door... but will their love prevail?

Also available as an audiobook.

Lightning Source UK Ltd.
Milton Keynes UK
UKHW011846041119
352881UK00019B/413/P